THE BOLO BATTALION

Westminster Press Books
by
Gordon D. Shirreffs

Action Front!
The Cold Seas Beyond
The Enemy Seas
The Hostile Beaches
Powder Boy of the *Monitor*
The Bolo Battalion

THE
BOLO
BATTALION

by
Gordon D. Shirreffs

THE WESTMINSTER PRESS
Philadelphia

LIBRARY OF CONGRESS CATALOG CARD NO. 66–17606

PUBLISHED BY THE WESTMINSTER PRESS ®
PHILADELPHIA, PENNSYLVANIA

PRINTED IN THE UNITED STATES OF AMERICA

To Robert S. Johnson,
friend, philosopher,
and fishing partner.

1 . . .

THE VETERAN United States submarine *Grayfin* surfaced
an hour after dusk in the rain-swept Sulu Sea somewhere south of Mindoro Island in the Philippines. The
sharklike prow reared itself out of the darkness of the
depths with a roar of cascading water. The long, dark
hull was leprous with rust and salt-encrusted sores. Even
before she leveled off at surface trim, with the water
foaming and streaming from her deck and freeing ports,
a hatch popped open with a rush of air.

Inside the conning tower the sound of the klaxon surfacing alarm died away, and as the hatch was opened at
the top of the ladder, a shower of water poured down to
be met by the onrush of officers and men scrambling to
reach their surface posts. Signalman Second Class Bob
Dunbar expertly swung up into his lookout ring abaft
the periscope shears, plugged in his rubberized telephone
line, uncased his night glasses and slung them about his
neck. He focused them on the dimly seen propeller guards
and then raised them to cover his prescribed arc of observation. It was only then that he realized it was raining—
a pounding tropical downpour with the hard-driven drops
hissing into the wrinkling slate-black sea. *Grayfin* rolled
a little uneasily, getting the feel of the tumbling seas.

She was a good sea boat despite her low freeboard, like all *Gato*-class fleet-type submarines.

Bob did not take his eyes from his night glasses, but all around him he could hear voices sounding off in the rigidly prescribed surfacing ritual. "Permission to start the turboblow, sir!" "Permission granted!" "Permission to charge batteries, sir!" "Permission granted!" The radar aerial was whirling steadily over Bob's head, peering into the darkness with invisible long-range eyes. The four diesel engines, nicknamed, Matthew, Mark, Luke, and John by Commander Gil Currie, skipper of *Grayfin*, had roared into life, spitting sharply and smokily through the exhausts on "All ahead, standard!"

"Permission to dump garbage, sir!" called out Gunner's Mate Third Class Gary Lunt, Bob's sidekick. "Permission granted!" The weighted bag plunged over the side into the dark foaming water that seemed to be racing past the sleek hull. Gary looked up at Bob for a fraction of a second and held up two fingers, nodding wisely. Then he vanished under the coldly watchful eye of the skipper on the little bridge.

Bob raised his glasses again. The usual scuttlebutt had begun to fill *Grayfin* at Port Darwin the moment she had cast loose from the submarine tender, with her wounds and scars tended to and her tanks topped off. Rumor had it that *Grayfin* was due for a "special mission," perhaps something like the one she had just completed off Borneo in enemy seas. But a special mission could mean a great many different things. Reconnaissance, supply, evacuation or rescue, transportation of coast watchers and intelligence agents, lifeguarding, mining, weather-reporting, minefield detection, anti-picket boat sweeps, shore bombardment, support of commando raids, or serving as marker beacons for surface ships all fell under the general category of special missions.

It hadn't taken long to find out which category they were due for when boxes, crates, and bags began to descend on *Grayfin* in a steady shower. Tons of supplies were stuffed into every available space. No spare torpedoes were carried; only the tubes were loaded, the space for the spare torpedoes being utilized for the supplies. There were tommy guns and shotguns, carbines and automatic rifles, with ammunition to match. Hand grenades, bazookas, jungle camouflage suits, GI suntans, jungle boots, cigarettes, canned Spam, Vienna sausages, and corned beef, cheese, atabrine, medical supplies, radios, generators, batteries, flashlights, and bulbs. *Grayfin* was obviously destined for a supply mission, but where was it to be?

Bob remembered all too well that they had had a rough time ashore on North Borneo on their last mission, one with a dual objective. The first was to bring off some Australian and British commandos who had been ashore on North Borneo for several years behind enemy lines; the second, to scout the Japanese naval base at Tawitawi. Bob had been a volunteer with *Grayfin*'s rescue party which had gone ashore on North Borneo to find the commandos, but when *Grayfin* had been unable to keep the rendezvous with them, they had been forced to find other means of transportation, which had been a story in itself. Later *Grayfin* had been severely pounded by several depth-charge attacks before she had managed to expend all her torpedoes and come home with a broom lashed to her periscope shears, for she had accounted for seven enemy vessels, sweeping the enemy seas off Tawitawi.

As to the present mission, speculation had been rife aboard *Grayfin*. To climax it, one dark night four officers arrived on the wharf and were hurried aboard. Three of them were Army officers, of which two were Filipinos, and the fourth was a naval officer. The Filipinos spoke perfect English, and Bob had heard all four of them conversing in Spanish as well as Tagalog. It was Stan Blascovitz, the head cook, who had recognized the Tagalog from his prewar service at Cavite in Manila Bay. From the moment the four passengers arrived, *Grayfin* had been filled to overflowing with scuttlebutt. Every crewman eyed those four officers, as well as their own, for the slightest clue as to *Grayfin*'s destination, but it never came.

They had left Port Darwin under sealed orders and knew they were to supply the "underground" war in the Philippines; but there were many islands great and small in the Philippine Archipelago, and their destination could be any one of them. U.S. submarines had never surrendered Philippine waters to the enemy. Even when the guns were still slamming on Guadalcanal in January of 1943, submarines had begun to land intelligence agents and supplies on the islands of Negros, Mindanao, Mindoro, Basilan, Panay, and Luzon, as well as other islands where guerrillas still held out.

Grayfin rolled heavily, plunging her bows deep into the dark seas. It was getting rougher. The rain seemed to smash down on the sea. It made hard going, but also was good cover for the stealthy approach of the submersible. No one knew her destination except the skipper and the four mysterious officers who were passengers. That was why Gary Lunt, cook's striker and undisputed commanding officer of the garbage-dumping detail when he wasn't manning a 20mm. with professional skill, had mysteriously held up two fingers to Bob before he had gone below. Their various unknown destinations had been given numbers. Number One was Mindanao, Two was Negros, Three was Panay, Four was Mindoro, and Five was Luzon. Evidently the guesswork was now in favor of Negros.

Bob scanned the rain-lashed seas. Somewhere off to starboard would be Negros, but there was no way of guessing *Grayfin's* course in this kind of weather. It had been a long trip from Port Darwin through the Timor Sea, then right to the Arafura Sea, up past the Moluccas, the Spice Islands, veering left almost to Borneo—of evil and unpleasant memory to the men of the *Grayfin*—then running on through the Celebes Sea into the Sulu Sea in the very heart of the many and widely scattered islands of the Philippine Archipelago.

Whitish, ghostly-looking spray showered back against the rust-scaled, salt-crusted conning tower. Now and then she drove on into rainless areas and another vicious squall would sweep swiftly across the dark waters trying to drive the heaving waves flat.

Two of the passengers came up onto the cigarette deck on the after part of the conning tower, just below Bob's post. They wore borrowed foul-weather gear. One of them was a Filipino and the other an American, but they were talking in low voices in some kind of Filipino dialect. They clung to the railing, peering out into the wet and windy darkness. Soon they would be taken ashore somewhere out there, thought Bob, and landed on some unnamed beach with their tons of supplies to vanish by daylight into the thick jungle, *if* the Japanese did not spot them first. Bob shivered. He had had enough of land warfare in the Aleutians, the Solomons, and on North Borneo. He grinned to himself. In many ways his naval service had been more amphibious than strictly seagoing; more like a gyrene than a swab jockey. His land duty had seemed to be a constant struggle to stay a hop, skip, and a jump ahead of the Japanese.

Ensign Tolliver had told him there were thousands of guerrillas in the many islands of the Philippines, many of them American Army and Navy personnel who had been cut off from escape and had managed to stay out of Japanese hands. They had started guerrilla warfare on their own with no Mamma, no Papa, and no Uncle Sam. The principal, well-organized guerrilla forces, usually led by high-ranking American officers, were on Luzon, Mindoro, and Mindanao. These forces were composite ones of American and Filipino service personnel, aided by "Bolo Battalions" of civilian Filipinos, as well as some of the native tribes who had no use for the Japanese. Some Filipinos, however, had joined the constabulary organized by the Japanese—the BC. The war had developed into a savage give-and-take, with no quarter asked and none given.

Grayfin was in dangerous waters, well patrolled by enemy air and surface craft as well as by submarines. No one was sure how many of these craft were equipped with radar, or how good it was. The darkness and the pounding tropical rain were heaven-sent, but they could not stop the probing fingers of enemy radar. Bob glanced up at the whirling radar of *Grayfin*. She, too, was sending out invisible feelers from radar and sound gear. Submarine radar and sonar ratings were the best in the business. They *had* to be, for the life of the submarine often depended upon them, as it was depending upon them now.

Bob impatiently flicked rainwater and spray from his face and peered into the downpour. He felt that he wasn't doing a bit of good, but he enjoyed being out in the weather again. After days of running submerged, he looked forward to the nights when *Grayfin* ran on the surface to charge her massive batteries and to make faster time. They were getting close to their unknown destination. Bob felt uneasy as he thought of *Grayfin* moving in close to a dangerous, uncharted shore, looking for the secretive signals from the guerrillas. Once close into shore in shallow water, with her hatches wide open while she discharged her cargo, *Grayfin* would be helpless. One submarine had been lost that way earlier in 1944, shattered and split open like a dropped melon when she had been caught by Japanese aircraft. Most of her crew had not survived. Some of them still lay in her rusted, shattered hulk and the others had long since vanished into the Philippine jungle, and no one knew whether any of them were alive or dead. But the Bamboo Warriors, the guerrilla fighters, needed supplies, and submarines were the only way to get them into the islands. As Gary Lunt had once cheerfully said, "Well, ol' *Grayfin* has paid for herself about now and from here on she's expendable."

Grayfin pitched and rolled a little wildly in the grip of a cross sea. Spray and waves dashed high above her plunging bullnose, sweeping back over the slotted wooden decking to wash hard against the base of the conning tower, and then climbing high enough to smash down on the little bridge. *Grayfin* dipped deeply and rolled a little, and Bob took his eyes from his glasses with an uneasy premonition in his mind. Tons of churning water roared up onto the deck and rose above the bridge to drop down with stunning, insensate force. Bob let his glasses hang from the strap as he clutched for handholds under the deluge of water. The main engine exhausts popped and crackled. As the surging water cleared the decking, *Grayfin* lost headway and rolled sluggishly. The main exhausts no longer spat out fumes and smoke. Suddenly thick black smoke gushed out of the fair-weather main ventilation duct.

Bob could hear the report that rattled tinnily up onto the bridge from the speaker. "Water flooded the main induction and stopped all main propulsion, Skipper. It came through an opening in the ventilation and shorted out the battery switches in the maneuvering room. The

13

wiring caught on fire. Water and salt got into the battery cells under the sleeping compartment, and some of the men caught a bad dose of smoke and fumes. We're covering the battery area with wet blankets to keep down the fumes. Fire is being brought under control."

The submarine wallowed uneasily as she lost headway and turned away from the pounding seas, taking sea after sea across her low-lying hull. In a short time she began to move ahead again under her two main engines, advancing heavily and slowly through the increasing seas.

One of the thoroughly soaked Army officers looked up at Bob with a quizzical smile. "Is it always like this, sailor?" he asked.

"Sometimes worse," said Bob.

The second officer was a Filipino. He hunched down into his foul-weather jacket and looked up into the streaming darkness. "If this keeps on," he said thoughtfully, "the jungle trails will be thick with mud. It will not be easy to get the supplies up off the beach before the dawn comes. I do not like this, Phil."

The American jerked his head. "*Bahála ná*, Freddie," he said. "We've got to risk it. We can't go back now."

Bob looked curiously at him. "*Bahála ná?*" he asked.

Phil shrugged and held out his hands, palms upward, with a comical look of resignation on his lean and handsome face. "*Bahála ná.* Come what may. If you spend much time in these islands, kid, it'll be an expression you'll hear every day and it won't be long before you'll be using it yourself."

Bob caught a hard look from Ensign Tolliver on the bridge. He turned quickly to the binoculars. He should have known better than to take his attention away from his duty. The safety of the boat and crew might depend on his watchfulness.

14

"The rivers will be badly swollen," said Frederico Campos, the Filipino officer.

"*Bahála ná*," said Phil.

"The carabaos will have a hard time getting through the mud of the trails."

"*Bahála ná.*"

Frederico grinned, revealing his even white teeth. "Now I know why I asked for you to come back with me. Even a Filipino cannot say *bahála ná* with such expression and *mean* it as well."

The two officers went below. Bob kept sweeping his observation arc with the night glasses, but his mind continually strayed. They had said dawn. That would be a matter of perhaps nine or ten hours. They were somewhere south of Mindoro, but he had no idea how *far* south they were. They couldn't make top speed of seventeen knots in these seas, and with only the two main engines driving *Grayfin* on, it wasn't likely they'd make a landfall on Mindoro. It might be Negros. But then they had not said *which* dawn. He shrugged. *Bahála ná!* He had been in this man's Navy too long to sweat out the imponderables, but still . . .

He was duly relieved from his watch and went below. He got in his full four hours of sleep and was awakened to stand sonar watch. He was a striker, or learner, under Sonarman First Class Eddie Scarlotti. There was enough time to put a strain on the coffee urn. Getting his steaming cup of joe, Bob sat down at the mess table just as Gary came out of the galley and looked about with a conspiratorial air.

"Well?" said Gary as he sat down opposite Bob.

Bob sipped his coffee. "You know I don't know any more than you do, Mac."

"You were on watch when those two Army fellows were

15

talking, weren't you?" asked Gary. "Is it Mindoro?"

Stan Blascovitz came out of the galley. He dropped into a seat and looked wearily at Gary. "I'm telling this meatball again and again it's *not* Mindoro," he said patiently.

Bob eyed the cook. "What's your choice, Blas?"

Blascovitz looked quickly from one side to the other and then behind him.

"You didn't look under the table," said Bob dryly.

"Yeh," said Blas. He peered under the table.

Bob rolled his eyes upward.

Blas raised his head. "It's not Mindoro!"

"Where is it then?" asked Bob.

Once again the head swung from side to side and then back.

"Under the table," prompted Bob.

Blas obediently looked under the table.

Bob grinned. "Come on, Blas," he pleaded.

"It's Manila Bay," said Blas in a hushed tone. "By Godfrey! Right in past ol' Corregidor and right on into Cavite."

"Well," said Gary, "I've heard everything now."

Blas gripped Gary by the wrist so hard that Blas's huge right biceps expanded, giving a fuller view of the pierced and bleeding heart tattooed on it, with the inscription below *What Is Home Without a Mother?* Blas looked about again. "I heard that Filipino officer Campos say something to the one named Phil," he said mysteriously. "I recognized the name of the place. I was at Cavite in thirty-eight on one of the old Sugar Boats, the S-32. I could speak the language pretty well, if I do say so myself. Well, I recognized these two words, see? I tell you fellows, ol' Blas *knows* now."

"What were the two words?" said Bob curiously.

Once again the head turned left, right, back, and then

16

popped under the table. Blas raised his huge head. "*Bahála ná!*" he said triumphantly.

To Bob's everlasting credit he did not crack the faintest trace of a smile. "*Bahála ná?*" he said thoughtfully. He stroked his chin.

"Yeh!" said Blas. "That's right near ol' Cavite!"

"Big place?" said Bob.

Blas waved a hamlike hand. "Middling," he said. He tilted his head and looked at Bob with suspicion. "You ever hear of it?"

Bob nodded. "Yup."

"So I'm right, hey?"

"So you're wrong, hey," said Bob. He stood up and drained his coffee cup. He was due on sonar watch. "*Bahála ná* isn't on Manila Bay. It isn't even on Luzon. It's on Sarangani Island. I heard the skipper say so." He vanished as quickly as he could while Gary ran to get Blas's dog-eared atlas, which he had bought for a shilling in a Port Darwin shop.

Bob was at the sonar set with his earphones on, trying to pick out and identify various sounds when he happened to look past Eddie Scarlotti and saw the broad, round face of Stan Blascovitz peering fixedly at him like a basilisk from the after end of the control room. Stan's lips formed the words Sarangani Island and then he cut the edge of his right hand sharply across his throat and vanished as silently as he had appeared, like some malevolent and brooding monster of the deep. Bob laughed. Sarangani Island was off the southernmost tip of Mindanao, at least five hundred miles south of *Grayfin's* estimated position and in the opposite direction from which she was heading.

2 . . .

S TAND BY to surface!" cracked out the voice of Commander Currie, and almost instantaneously the klaxon blared. "Lookouts! Stand by to surface!" *Grayfin* slanted upward. "Lookouts in the conning tower! Shift to all four diesels! All ahead standard!" The hatch popped open with a weird whistling of air, and water showered down. The low-pressure blowers began to squeal, the pitch rising higher and higher through the still-revolving fans after the valves had been secured. The diesels roared into life.

Bob Dunbar swung up into his lookout post. It was dark, with a soft velvety quality to the night and the smoothly rising waves. The exhausts crackled, popped, and smoked as sixty-four cylinders drove *Grayfin* through the smooth waters, parting them easily, leaving a spreading white wake far behind the submarine. A wraith of exhaust smoke drifted aft in the windless air. Bob swung his glasses, and his heart leaped. They were heading in toward a low-lying shore. There wasn't a light to be seen. The darkness was thick as though a heavily wooded area, probably swamp or jungle, was beyond the shoreline, where the land seemed to rise gradually to greater heights, but Bob could not differentiate between the heights and the darkness of the night sky.

Grayfin had rested on the bottom all that day, with the depth-gauge needle fixed at one hundred and fifty feet. An air of tenseness and expectancy had hung within the boat during those long hours. They had all known that they were waiting for nightfall in order to make their approach, and that before the coming dawn while tons of supplies were being removed from *Grayfin* she would be absolutely helpless. How many hours would it take?

The dull black hull would be difficult, if not impossible, to see against the dark waters; but the wake was white and very wide, and the sound of the diesels would carry far in the windless night. Bob wet his dry lips. It must be Mindoro they were approaching. He glanced toward the bridge at the dim faces of the officers. Lieutenant Frederico Campos was on the bridge beside Commander Currie, looking steadfastly toward the land. The radar whirled steadily. The lookouts never stopped probing into the darkness with their powerful night glasses.

There might be A/S craft out there in the darkness, or perhaps a Japanese picket submarine, echo-ranging and radar-scanning. There might be patrol planes up in the pitchy night, their engines unheard because of the noise of *Grayfin's* diesels. It was an eerie, itchy feeling that came over the men on the deck of the submarine. At that they probably felt less tense than the men inside the boat, who couldn't see into the darkness but who had to remain at their posts, performing the myriad functions that kept *Grayfin* moving in toward her destination.

The bridge speaker squawked. A command cracked out. The annunciators tinkled faintly, and the roaring of the diesels died away. *Grayfin* moved ahead on momentum alone, with the sea washing against her sides. Then she lost headway and drifted. A faint sound came through the overhead darkness—the intermittent humming of an engine. Bob felt the cold sweat break out on his body. He raised his glasses to look up toward the sound. It was useless. He couldn't see a thing.

The sound of the plane came closer. Bob tried to convince himself that it would take powerful glasses to spot the lean, dark-colored hull against the dark waters now that the wake wasn't visible; but the plane just might have radar or might be working on a radar bearing transmitted by radio from a patrol craft or perhaps a shore station.

The sound became louder and louder, and Bob could have sworn the plane was dropping in altitude. He raised the glasses again and caught a faint, flickering bluish light. "Bridge!" he snapped. "Engine exhausts bearing two-eight-oh!"

"Bridge, aye, aye," came back the calm voice of Commander Currie.

Bob swallowed. The plane was swinging in a wide arc, dropping rapidly in altitude. Then it leveled off and flew right at *Grayfin*. The roaring of the engine increased, with that peculiar intermittent sound some Japanese engines had. Bob could almost feel those enemy eyes peering down at him through excellent Japanese night glasses.

Grayfin was dead in the water, rolling gently, the seas gurgling and slobbering through the freeing ports.

"Don't look up at it!" snapped the skipper.

White faces might be spotted from that height against the darkness of the deck. It was rougher on the nerves not to look at the approaching plane as it roared closer and closer, and then it was right on them, sweeping overhead at about a two-hundred-foot altitude. It flew straight on along the dark coastline, and in a little while the sound of the engine died away.

"Slow ahead," came the command.

The annunciators tinkled. The diesels crackled into life. *Grayfin* began to fashion a wake again.

An hour drifted past, and another. The shore loomed

closer but it was still dark and seemingly lifeless. Commander Currie took some careful bearings and looked at Lieutenant Campos. He nodded. Campos raised a signaling tube and rested it on the rail of the bridge. Bob could not see the spot of light flicking off and on within the tube that shielded it from sideway vision.

"Lookouts scan the shoreline," said the skipper.

Bob studied the dark line of the coast. A pinpoint of light showed, flicking rapidly on and off. Bob was a signalman, an expert, but the dots and dashes meant nothing to him except a string of unrelated letters. The light went out.

Campos nodded at Commander Currie. *Grayfin* moved on.

The shoreline was pitch-dark again. The sound of the diesels seemed inordinately loud. Bob nearly leaped out of his lookout ring when a light snapped on, then off, not two hundred yards dead ahead of the submarine. He was about to call out when he heard Lieutenant Campos speak. "That is the *caba-caba*," he said. "A small banca."

"Gee, thanks, Freddie," said Commander Currie. "I'm glad you told me a *caba-caba* is a small banca. Now all I have to do is find out what a banca is."

The white teeth of the Filipino showed in the darkness. "A banca is a boat hollowed from a big log, with outrigger. A *caba-caba* is a smaller boat hollowed from a smaller log. *¿Comprende?*"

"Now I know everything," said the skipper.

The light flicked on just ahead of the submarine. "All stop," came the command. The roaring of the diesels died away across the dark waters. *Grayfin* still moved toward the unseen *caba-caba*. A soft voice hailed out of the darkness. Lieutenant Campos replied in the native tongue.

Bob saw the log boat bobbing up and down in the water. Three men were in it. The single sail flapped in the gently rising offshore wind. *"Oi* there! *Oi!"* one of the men called out. He cast a heaving line toward the submarine, which was caught by a seaman and made fast. The *caba-caba* bumped against the side of *Grayfin* and one of the men scrambled onto the deck, aided by the seaman. The line was cast loose and the *caba-caba* drifted off. The two men began to paddle it toward the unseen shore with a faint bluish light shielded on the bobbing stern.

Bob could hear the men conversing on the bridge. "This is Mang Pedro, sir. He says his English is not too good. I will translate," said Lieutenant Campos. "He will pilot us in."

Commander Currie nodded. "Just the same, I want a man in the chains with a lead line."

The seaman on deck ran forward with the lead line swinging in his hand. "Slow ahead," came the command. *Grayfin* moved after the faint bluish light. Now and then the old man on the bridge would say something in his native tongue, translated by Lieutenant Campos, and the *Grayfin's* course would be shifted a little.

"No bottom!" called out the leadsman.

The old man spoke quickly. "He says the bottom shelves rapidly in two hundred yards," said Campos.

"Is there a pier or wharf, or anything like that?" asked the skipper. He listened to the old man speaking to Campos.

"He says everything will be fine, sir. Oh, yes, sir, everything No. 1, first class," said Campos. He grinned. "It is not necessary to fear. Oh, no, sir."

"Ask him about the Japanese."

Campos spoke to Mang Pedro and then translated his answer. "He says the Hapons, that's the Japanese, have been suspicious, but they have not come near this place. There was a boat offshore late this afternoon, and several planes."

22

"No bottom!" called out the leadsman.

"Mister Tolliver, sir," said Commander Currie, "have the gun crews man the guns, if you please."

The gun crews tumbled up on deck, working swiftly in the darkness with long-practiced skill. They wore life jackets and steel helmets. The ammunition hatch was opened and shells passed up. The 20mm. guns were readied, one of them having Gary Lunt as gunner, and despite his lackadaisical, happy-go-lucky attitude, Gary had already accounted for several Japanese planes.

"Deck gun manned and ready, sir!"

"20mm.'s manned and ready, sir!"

Ensign Tolliver had added a touch of his own. Four men appeared on deck, two of them carrying tommy guns and the other two armed with BAR's, the heavy and accurate Browning automatic rifle.

"By the mark twelve," came back the singsong voice of the leadsman.

Grayfin nosed on after the dim bluish light. She just about had steerageway on her.

"By the mark eleven!" came back the chant. "By the deep ten!"

"We're drawing eighteen feet at this trim, sir," said Lieutenant Jenkins.

"Aye, aye," said the skipper.

"And a half nine! By the mark nine!"

Mang Pedro spoke softly, and the helm was moved to angle the submarine a little to starboard. Almost at once the *caba-caba* took the same course. The old man must know that channel like the palms of his wrinkled old hands. The old man spoke again. "There are bamboo fish traps here," said Campos.

The hull scraped gently against something. A float bobbed up and down in the dark waters.

"By the deep eight! And a half seven! By the mark

eight! By the mark eight! And a half seven! By the mark seven! And a half six!" chanted the leadsman.

Again came the scraping as the bamboo fish traps raked along the side of the hull. Mang Pedro spoke again. The helm was shifted. A fraction of a moment later the bluish light shifted as well. They could have forgotten about the *caba-caba* and the bluish light, thought Bob.

"By the deep six! By the mark six! By the deep five. By the mark five and shoaling fast!"

Bob swept the darkness with his glasses. He could make out a thick growth of trees with a lighter patch of beach in front of it. It seemed uncomfortably close.

"By the mark four!"

Bob swallowed hard. Twenty-four feet deep. *Grayfin* was trimmed at eighteen. Six feet of water under her keel . . .

Mang Pedro spoke. Campos translated swiftly. "All stop," said Commander Currie. Bob could see the sweat glistening on Lieutenant Jenkins' face. It looked as if *Grayfin* might have to wade in.

"Boats, sir," called back the leadsman. "Dozens of 'em!"

All sorts of small boats bobbed in the wash of the gentle surf. Most of them had been lashed together in pairs. The water seemed covered with them.

Mang Pedro spoke quickly. Campos repeated what he had said. The anchor plunged into the shallow water with a loud rattling of chain that stridently echoed and re-echoed from the shoreline. Bob could have sworn the sound would carry all the way to Manila. Hatches banged open and a faint bluish light came from within the submarine. The crew began to heave boxes up onto the deck.

As soon as Bob's nose got rid of the odor of the exhausts, he noticed the almost overpowering land smell that drifted out and seemed to settle about *Grayfin* like a cloak. It had a sweetish and yet a sort of musty odor to it. It reminded

24

him of someplace, and then he recalled where it had been —in the Solomons. He had had his fill of the jungle there and on North Borneo.

The double boats were filled dangerously deep with cargo and paddled off into the darkness while empty ones took their places. There was no talking. There were no commands. Yet every man seemed to know exactly what to do. Once in a while there would be a soft whistle or a hand motion, but that was about all. The loaded boats seemed to be swallowed up as they were paddled toward the faint line of beach.

Every man aboard the *Grayfin* who was not on duty below, or passing up the cargo to the deck, was on deck, peering up into the sky, or out to sea. If their boat was caught, it would be a sitting duck. As fast as the cargo was moving, it seemed agonizingly slow to Bob. Now and then he looked at the dim face of Gary beneath the helmet brim. Gary was in the ring of his gun, the slender barrel tilted up toward the dark sky, watching and listening for a patrol plane.

Grayfin would have to be emptied at least an hour before the dawn so as to be able to work her way back through the channel and the encroaching fish traps. Why didn't they hurry up! It was already well past midnight and still the unloading went on and on. The sight of the pairs of boats being placed alongside the hull, to be filled, then to shove off, to be instantly replaced by another pair, began to mesmerize Bob. All the boats and all the Filipinos seemed to look exactly alike. Once a light flicked on and then off at the edge of the jungle, and Bob estimated that they were about two hundred yards from the shore.

Gary Lunt raised his head. Bob glanced at him. Gary had superb hearing. He narrowed his eyes. "Sounded like an airplane motor," he called out.

Commander Currie whirled. "Can you hear it now?"

Gary shook his head. All the lookouts trained their glasses in the direction to which Gary was pointing. Bob could see nothing. But, if the Japanese had cut his engine, there'd be no exhaust flames to see. He felt cold all over.

"Quiet out there!" called out Frederico Campos. He was the only one of the four passengers still aboard. The others had already been ferried ashore. Commander Currie had kept him aboard as translator.

The loading noises stopped. The wind rustled through the palm trees on shore, and the surf washed in and withdrew with a dragging, rumbling sound. Now and then a *caba-caba* bumped against the side of the submarine. A man coughed. Nothing else could be heard. Commander Currie opened his mouth to order the unloading to continue.

Bob narrowed his eyes. He had caught a faint, almost imperceptible movement in the sky. For a moment he thought he was seeing things and then he opened his mouth to yell a warning. It was too late. The darkness was exploded into nothingness by an intense white light which revealed just above it the parachute that was swinging gently and slowly downward. A whitish glow exposed the tangled jungle, thickly mantled with growth, and the rising slopes beyond. It exposed the beach, covered with boxes, crates, bags, and hundreds of Filipinos. It exposed beached boats and those paddling between the beach and the submarine. Worst of all, it fully exposed the long dark hull of *Grayfin*.

"There he is!" yelled a lookout. He pointed at the Japanese two-motored plane. The plane cut in its engines and banked to turn away. The four-inch deck gun opened fire with a jarring slam and spat a gushing streamer of smoke and flame. The breech flicked open, and the shell casing bounced on the deck and was instantly kicked over the side. The plane banked again and came in fast, every

26

gun firing and flickering with eerie light. Another flare burst into life just as the first one struck the water. The gunfire of the plane churned across the water fifty feet to one side of *Grayfin* and stitched a line of death and destruction through the crowded swarm of small boats. Men shrieked as they dived over the sides into the lighted water. A small bomb burst in the water. A *caba-caba* went down with a gurgling rush. The deck gun slammed again and again, numbing the ears and half blinding the eyes of the men on the deck. The 20mm. guns rattled stridently into life, firing streamers of tracer up at the plane which now headed inland. It seemed to stagger a little in the air, then plunged down toward the beach, crashing right at the waterline and scattering flaming wreckage into the jungle.

"More planes!" screamed Frederico Campos.

Three more bimotored planes were coming in at terrific speed, following the line of the beach, but they weren't coming to scatter flares as the ill-fated pathfinder plane had done. They wanted that submarine! Bullets stitched across the water. Slugs clanged against the conning tower of the submarine. A lookout swung lifelessly in his ring. There was a burst of flame at the base of the conning tower.

"The ammunition is going!" yelled Stan Blascovitz, who served as loader on the deck gun. There was a shattering blast of flame and smoke. Fire licked up the side of the conning tower.

"Jump, you lookouts!" commanded the skipper. Two bomb bursts straddled the hull.

Bob dropped from his ring, batting out flames that licked up his clothing. He was trapped on the deck with flames between him and the conning tower. He dived cleanly over the side, just clearing the hull. He came up and saw one of the planes whirling downward, with one wing missing, debris and flames being scattered across the water. Flames were dancing crazily on the deck of the submarine. Man after man dived over the side, one of them screaming in agony as his clothing flared up about his face. His hair was alight.

The dying plane plunged toward the water. Bob swam as he had never swum before, looking back over his shoulder, positive that the plane was going to ride him piggyback down into the four fathoms beneath him. The plane smashed with stunning force into the water between Bob and the *Grayfin*, and a sheet of flame arose from the smoking water as oil and gasoline were scattered pell-mell.

Bob drove his way through the water, heading for the beach. He passed an overturned baroto but didn't stop for a rest. Suddenly his feet struck bottom and he pushed through the water toward the beach. Then the whirling, fiery wing of the plane hit the water and instantly there was a wide band of flame between Bob and the submarine where the oil and gasoline had ignited atop the water. Bob turned toward the shore again and fell over a body rolling in the light surf. He could hear the men who were trapped in the burning area screaming as they faced a horrible death. He looked back once. Somehow they had managed to get *Grayfin* under way. She was crawling astern, with flames still licking about the conning tower and the abandoned deck gun. Now and then a lone 20mm. would rattle. Once a BAR let go with a full clip.

The remaining two planes banked away and turned out to sea, then swung in again for the cold meat they were so positive they were going to get. *Grayfin* had reached a place where she could swing around with agonizing slowness. The very eagerness of the Japanese frustrated their own aims. One of them was forced to bank hard away to avoid hitting the other, and the remaining plane fell off on one wing. Bob could see hoses and foam lashing at the flames on the conning tower of the submarine. She was moving faster now, spreading a wider wake across the water. The deck gun flashed into life again and again. A 20mm. traced a line of fire across the sky, driving off one of the enemy planes. The parachute flare had long been out, but the flames from the ignited gasoline and oil on the water made the scene almost as bright as day.

Guns flashed and crackled from the beach as the Filipinos opened up on the planes. Bob waded ashore. Some of the newly landed supplies were ablaze. He joined a group of Filipinos who were throwing sand on the flames. One of them had a mask of blood on his face but he held the wound with one hand and cast sand with the other. Bob kept on heaving sand, but every so often he would look back over his shoulder. *Grayfin* was still racing out to sea at her full seventeen knots surface speed, trying to reach water deep enough to dive into. It shouldn't take her long, for the bottom shelved steeply. Her guns were flashing but the fire was out. The next time he looked back she was gone. The planes swung in to strafe the beach. Bob did not stand on the order of his going. He crashed through the tangled jungle and dived flat, right on top of a big Filipino.

"Sorry," he yelled.

A rounded, smoke-streaked face looked up at Bob. "It's all right, kid," said Stan Blascovitz. "Better you should land on ol' Uncle Stanley than land in this stinking muck I'm lying in." He wiped the sweat from his face. "Man, I came ashore fast with flames singeing my skivvies. Never knew Mrs. Blascovitz' favorite son Stanislaus was a Johnny Weissmuller. They get the *Grayfin?*" He looked anxiously at Bob.

Bob shook his head. "She got out to sea. They put out the fire. She must have dived as soon as she could."

Blascovitz rubbed his flattened nose with the back of a huge and hairy hand. *"Dived?"* he said in a faraway voice.

"Look, Blas, maybe she wasn't hurt bad," said Bob.

Blas nodded. "How many of the fellows did they get?"

Bob shrugged. "I saw three or four."

"Know any of them?"

"That replacement radioman we got at Port Darwin. Smythe, wasn't it? Jim Smythe?"

"Yeh," said the cook. "Nice kid. Lousy domino player, but a nice kid. They got one of those Filipino officers we had on board."

The planes were roaring off into the night. The flames had begun to die down. Filipinos finished putting out the fire among the supplies. Here and there in the water lifeless bodies drifted, rolling back and forth in the wash of the surf. A smell of smoke and fumes hung in the air.

Bob stood up and wiped his hands on his soaked trousers. "You see Gary?" he said quietly.

Blascovitz sat up and examined a cut on his hand. He did not look up. "No," he said.

A man pushed his way through the tangle. It was Lieutenant Campos. "Let's go," he said. "We've got to get off this beach. Japanese Marines have landed upshore a mile from here. Listen!"

The faint rattle of rifle and automatic weapon fire came to them, punctuated with the dull sound of a mortar burst.

Blascovitz stood up. "Where do we go, sir?" he asked.

Campos pointed to the jungle. "We can be at the rendezvous barrio by dawn," he said.

"That's inland," said Bob.

"That's right," said the officer.

"But the *Grayfin*," said Bob.

"She won't be back, kid," said Blascovitz. "We're a shore detail now." He hitched up his filthy pants. "Well, I served ashore at Cavite back in the thirties and I guess I can do a shore stretch again, but I never figured on doing it *this* way."

A line of men walked into the jungle carrying some of the supplies. Awkward-looking carabaos hauled creaking, sagging carts loaded with some of the smoke-blackened and charred containers. Frederico Campos handed Bob a rusty carbine and Stan a revolver. "Best I can do right now," he said. "We'll outfit you at the barrio. *Sigi legi, ho!* Shake a leg!" He turned and walked on after the others.

"Come on, Bob," said Blas.

Bob parted some of the growth and looked out across the darkening sea. The breeze had shifted, blowing in from the sea and dispelling the smoke with a fresh salty tang. There was no sign of anything atop the deeper water. Had *Grayfin* managed to escape, licking her wounds and burns, or had she gone down forever?

"Kid," said Blas, "we don't know the way. We could get lost in this jungle fairyland, like they write about in books."

Bob nodded and turned. *"Sigi legi, ho!"*

They followed the others. The musty, rank smell of the jungle closed in on them, and away from the shore breeze the heat was oppressive. Blas looked at Bob. "Mindoro, hey?"

Bob nodded.

They slogged on with the mud up to their shoe tops. Mosquitoes hummed in, ready for action. Sticky sweat began to trickle down their bodies. Bob shook his head. *"Bahála ná,"* he said.

3 . . .

THE SUN came up and began to pour tropical heat down onto the steaming jungle. Somewhere in the depths a conch shell blew a melancholy, far-reaching note that was held a long time. It was called a *bojong*, Bob had learned, and was used by the Filipinos for signaling, for it sounded almost exactly like a jungle bird.

Frederico Campos stood beside the trail watching the two sailors struggling along. "How does it go?" he asked.

Bob grinned weakly. "I'll make it, sir."

Blas wiped the sweat from his face. "Those *bojongs*," he said. "They blow them all the time, sir?"

The officer nodded. "Signaling." He shoved back his hat. "If the Japs catch you with one of them, they'll kill you on the spot."

"Jolly," said Bob. He heard the call once more. "There it goes again."

The officer shook his head. "That's a *bojong* bird. Sounds like a shell, but not quite the same. Japs can't tell them apart."

"Misleading, isn't it, sir?" said Blas.

The Filipino nodded. "Can't tell sometimes. The boys yell out to each other: 'Was that *your bojong* or a *bojong's bojong?*' "

"How did the fight on the beach come out?" Bob asked.

"Rough. Those Japanese Marines are tough babies. Our *boroba*—that's a guerrilla force—held them back long enough for us to *buqwee* out of there. That means to pull foot. Hightail it."

"Where'd you hear all that scuttlebutt, sir?" asked Blas. "Radio?"

Campos shook his head. "Bamboo Telegraph," he said.

"Any news of *Grayfin,* sir?" asked Bob.

A troubled look crossed the Filipino's face. "No," he said. "I'm sorry, men. Maybe she made it to deeper water."

"Yeh," said the cook. "Sure! Those Nip planes couldn't get the ol' *Grayfin.* Why, I mind the time we . . ." His voice trailed off. "It's no use," he added miserably.

They slogged on through rising, oppressive heat. There was a clammy, dragging feeling to their soaked clothing. The salt sting of sweat burned in their eyes. Nettles and sharp-edged grasses ripped at their legs and arms as they forced their way forward. The dank, musty, jungle smell engulfed them, and their hearts fluttered rapidly. Lieutenant Campos had told Bob everyone got that feeling in jungle marching. Between the sweat, blisters, nettles, and the enervating heat it didn't seem as though they could go on. Their hair felt as though it was plastered with mud, but it was only the sweat. Balls of sweat rolled down their backs like crawling bugs. And always, sometimes behind them or to either side, or sometimes ahead, came the long, melancholy, far-reaching notes of a *bojong.*

It was slow going. The carabaos had no natural cooling system in their tough hides and had to wallow for one half hour out of every four. The wallowing period was a godsend to Blas and Bob, for just about the time the carabaos had to wallow, so did the two *Grayfin* men.

Bob lay on his back, heedless of the smelly mud. The jungle was alive with life. Birds of brilliant plumage darted in and out of hideouts of delicate, orchidlike flowers. Little brown monkeys with weird faces peered curiously down at the guerrillas. The morning sun cast a rosy light on the river, which was almost concealed by overhanging vines and thousands of exotic blossoms of every imaginable color in the vines and the branches of the trees. Lianas were looped from tree to tree, festooned with blossoms. Hundreds of monkeys romped in the tall trees, chattering noisily and blinking in the sun. Morning choruses of trilling birds rose clear and beautiful over the chattering and the ceaseless droning of insects. The long air roots of the trees beside the river were slimey, dipping deep into the dark-green water in which lurked crocodiles. Now and then the humped eyes and rounded tip of a nose would show above the water as a crocodile speculated on whether or not he could get a carabao.

"Wonder if ol' Tarzan would like it here?" said Stan idly. He scraped a leech from a muscular calf with the edge of his sheath knife. He eyed the repulsive thing. "You think these babies pick us out for blood type, kid? Supposing a leech is another type than we are. Man, he could sure make himself sick, hey?"

"I couldn't care less," said Bob. He wiped the sweat from his face, thinking of standing lookout aboard *Grayfin* during the night surface runs, with a cool breeze playing through his hair. He slapped a mosquito and picked a squirming bug from his left ear.

"Keep up the ol' spirit, Roberto," said Blas.

"It isn't easy," Bob retorted. "I enlisted in this man's Navy because I liked ships and the sea. So I get a tin can mined under me in the Solomons and end up on shore in Foofoofarongo, the Devil's Island of the South Pacific. Then I get on a PT by a stroke of sheer luck, and she takes off when a Jap can chases her, leaving Gary and me to end up coast-watching in the jungle. That was a *jungle*, Blas."

34

"Nothing as good as this, hey?"

Bob shrugged. "You see one jungle, Blas, you've seen 'em all."

"Then we picked you and Gary up after you got washed off your tin can in that typhoon earlier this year," said Blas. "I remember it as though it was yesterday. Man, how that kid could eat!" He grinned. "Come to think of it, you and Gary spent a little time ashore on North Borneo. Almost left you fellows behind there. I nearly had the crew back on regular rations because I didn't have to make allowances for Lunt."

Bob nodded. He clasped his hands behind his neck. They had thought the U.S.S. *Logie*, the tin can they had been washed off of, had been lost in the typhoon, but she hadn't. She had been badly damaged and had been sent back to Pearl for repairs—maybe even Frisco. Bob sighed. He and Gary had remained aboard *Grayfin*. He liked submarine duty, but he was having the same trouble with submarines that he had had with destroyers—*staying* on them.

"You shoulda been a Marine," said Blas. He rolled his eyes upward. "Perish the thought! That was a nasty thing to say to a nice kid like you."

"Oh, they have their uses," said Bob.

Blas looked at a sad-faced monkey who was watching him. "Yeh? Like what?"

"Like making amphibious landings, Blas. Little things like that. You know—Guadalcanal."

Blas nodded. He eyed the curious monkey. "I think he likes me, Bob."

"Maybe he thinks you're a relative."

Blas chuckled. "He looks better than *some* of my relatives. Man, you ought to see my cousin Eugene. Whoeee!"

A Filipino came and squatted beside them in the mud. He handed them some bread. "Good, sirs," he said with a pleasing smile. "Oh, very good indeed. *Poto sicle.* Baked rice bread. It is necessary to eat, sirs, to keep up the strength."

Blas opened his huge mouth to bite the bread and then he closed it again. "Can't sit here eating like a pig with cousin Eugene up there looking like that at me. It's hardly fitting."

The Filipino glanced up. "You desire the monkey for food, sir?"

"God forbid! That would be cannibalism."

The Filipino looked curiously at him. "Very good eating, sir."

Blas shook his head. He smiled at the monkey and the monkey smiled back, or at least Bob *thought* he did.

"One desires this monkey?" asked the Filipino.

Blas nodded solemnly. "One does."

The Filipino walked over to his pack and withdrew an empty coconut shell with a small hole cut in it, and with a cord attached to it. He took a piece of *poto sicle* and dropped it into the shell. Then he placed the shell at the foot of the tree where Eugene sat watching him with interest. The Filipino walked over to Blas and Bob and squatted beside them with the cord in his hand. "Do not look at him, sirs," he said. Minutes ticked past. Eugene came down the tree. He looked both ways and then thrust his tiny hand into the hole to grasp the food. The Filipino stood up and slowly began to pull the coconut to him with the cord. Eugene was being dragged behind the shell by his hand.

"Open your fist, you dummy!" said Bob.

The Filipino smiled. "He will not let loose of food once he has grasped it, sirs. That is why we catch them so easily." He grasped Eugene, avoiding the sharp teeth, and smashed the shell with the back edge of his bolo. Eugene

36

crammed the *poto sicle* into his mouth. The Filipino tied a loop of cord around Eugene's neck and handed the other end of the cord to Blas.

Three sharp, staccato notes carried through the jungle. They sounded twice more. The Filipinos hurried the wallowing carabaos out of the river and in among the trees. Bob looked up at the tall tree from which the signal had come. He could barely make out the Filipino hidden up there among the leaves. The man placed a flutelike instrument to his lips, and the sharp, staccato signal came again, echoing along the river.

"Scatter!" yelled Frederico Campos. *"Sigi legi, ho!"*

Bob ran for the underbrush. Stan followed clumsily, with Eugene hanging onto his neck with tiny brown arms. Bob couldn't help grinning. Eugene surely *had* recognized kinfolk. They crouched in the underbrush and looked out. The riverbank was clear. Above the shrieking of the nervous white cockatoos and the chattering of the monkeys came the distant intermittent humming sound of an airplane engine. The sound of the cockatoos and monkeys died away. Once more came the staccato signal. Then it was very quiet except for the rustling of the treetops in the hot wind, the occasional splashing of a crocodile in the river, and the sound of the engine coming closer and closer.

"He's following the river," said Frederico Campos.

No one moved and none of them looked up. The jungle was thick, but there were open spaces where a Japanese observer might spot a Filipino or a cart. He was evidently flying low.

"There he is," said Stan.

It was a twin-float plane, the bright yellow pontoons glistening in the sunlight. It swung from side to side as the pilot worked the stick so that the observer might see over either side with his powerful binoculars. The sun glinted from the long glass greenhouse atop the fuselage.

"Kawanishi 97," said Bob.

Campos nodded. "They use a lot of them around here. Too slow for the other combat zones. They can make plenty of trouble, though."

The plane dipped a little, and a fat yellow bomb dropped swiftly toward the river. The plane banked and flew off, gaining altitude. The bomb struck the river, raising a shimmering veil of water, and the river bottom seemed to erupt. Bob saw a flailing, bloody crocodile rise from the depths and land on the bank, thrashing about in its death spasms. Water rushed toward the bank and over-flowed it. The crashing echo of the bomb fled down the river aisle. A stench of rotting vegetation, mud, explosives, and smoke hung in the air.

"He see us?" said Bob.

Stan spat to one side. "Naw, he's just beating the brush, hoping to kick something out. Hey, Eugene?"

The monkey chattered. Stan listened to him solemnly.

"What's he saying?" asked Bob.

Stan held up a huge hand. "Don't interrupt! Go on, Eugene."

"He sure is windy."

Stan nodded. "He wants to know what a couple of sub-marine swabbies are doing fooling around in the jungle with a Bolo Battalion."

"A good question," said Bob. The thought of Gary struck him out of nowhere as the signal was given for the march to continue. They had been together a long time. Raised as kids together, going through high school together in Alaska. Serving aboard Bob's uncle's government-chartered craft, the *Otter*, during the Aleutian Campaign, enlisting together in the Navy and serving aboard the U.S.S.

MacRonan in the Solomons Campaign until she struck a mine. Serving on temporary duty aboard a PT boat, and later as voluntary coast watchers in the Solomons. They had served together aboard another tin can, the U.S.S. *Logie*, in the Marshalls, and later aboard the submarine U.S.S. *Grayfin* off North Borneo. They had stayed aboard *Grayfin* for their second war patrol to the Philippines. Maybe Gary's luck had at last run out.

Blas raised his head. "Eugene likes you, kid," he said.

Bob looked at him as he pushed himself wearily to his feet. A blister broke on his heel as he took his first step. "Thanks," he said. The misery on his face was plain enough to see. Even Eugene noticed it. He stopped chattering and watched Bob with his wise little face.

Blas stood up and settled the monkey on his shoulder. "They didn't get Gary, kid," he said.

"Yeh," said Bob. He wiped the sweat from his face.

"I thought maybe I saw him on *Grayfin* when she was backing out, Bob."

Bob looked back at the cook. "No, you didn't, Blas. Thanks anyway." He trudged off along the muddy trail, his carbine slung across his shoulder.

Blas looked at Eugene. "You've got to help cheer him up, Cousin," he said. "Understand?"

Eugene chattered on and on. Blas followed Bob. Along the edge of the mud-stained river a few Filipinos were softly singing as they gathered some of the fish the Hapons had so kindly supplied for them.

Frederico Campos trudged beside Bob. He pointed at the fish gatherers. "Hunger is the first enemy of any army, Bob," he said quietly. "We fight for supplies here on Mindoro. We seldom win any battles. We fight until we run out of ammunition, which is almost all the time, or until the Hapons successfully deploy against us. We are a hole-in-the-pants, banana-for-dinner army here on Mindoro, and most of the time we have nothing to fight with but our naked hearts. But we will not surrender, Bob. Never! Justice is with us and God goes with justice."

Bob looked sideways at the lean and handsome face of the officer. There was nothing dramatic about Frederico Campos. He had said it simply, because he meant it from the heart. He watched the officer hurry up the line of slowly moving carts to help free a wheel from the thick mud, heaving and straining with the others. General MacArthur had said, "I shall return." He would find that many brave Filipinos and Americans were waiting for him, and that they had kept up the good fight with faith that MacArthur *would* return.

The sun vanished behind a thick bank of clouds in the early afternoon, and soon thereafter heavy raindrops began to rattle on the leaves of the trees. Then the sluice gates of heaven let go in a pounding, smashing downpour of rain that struck like needles on the bare flesh and soaked everyone to the skin. In a matter of minutes the already muddy trail became a sticky, clinging morass. The water began to rise over the banks of the river and flood onto the trail as the convoy slogged on through the downpour. Bob had never seen anything like this rain, either in the cold and wet Aleutians or in the steaming jungles of the Solomons. It was like a vicious, malevolent living thing that seemed determined, in an insensate way, to smash the jungle growths flat into the mud along with Filipinos, carabaos, and carts, and to raise the rivers to meet the muck of the bottomland, transforming all of Mindoro into one vast lifeless, quaking morass, as it had been in primeval days.

The swirling water raised the tangled vines from the jungle floor and whipped them about the legs of the

40

struggling men and beasts so that they tripped and fell into the water and mud. Half the time they did not know whether they were wading or swimming. Logs swirled in from the river, driving butt ended at the legs of the men and carabaos or slamming sideways into them with massive force. A carabao went down with two broken legs, and the Filipino driver pulled back its head and slashed his razor-sharp bolo across the taut, distended throat muscles. The blood gushed into the muddy water, turning it into a pinkish flood. Before the convoy went on, after unloading the stalled cart and distributing the load among the others, most of the meat of the dead carabao had been slashed from it. As Frederico Campos had said, "Hunger is the first enemy of any army."

The water rose knee-deep, then thigh-deep and then hip-deep, forming eddies about the thick boles of the trees, casting matted tangles of lianas across the trail that was now but an extension of the roaring river. Mang Pedro, the Filipino, led the way toward higher ground. Frederico Campos said the old man was over seventy years of age. The prefix "Mang" to his name indicated a sign of respect for an old man of wisdom and experience. He had been a sergeant in the Philippine Scouts over forty years past, and had been a friend to the father of General Douglas MacArthur. He was a legend on Mindoro.

They reached the higher ground with the loss of but one more carabao, who was duly cut up for meat in two feet of muddy water. They squatted in the glutinous mud or leaned against trees, watching the rapidly rising water with patient eyes. One thing was certain. In such weather the Hapons could not fly, nor could they pursue them up the flooded trails.

Bob stood watching Stan Blascovitz, who was talking to Eugene. *"Bahála ná,"* said Bob.

41

Stan nodded. "It's got a lot more meaning to me now, kid."

The rain eased off, but water still flooded the trail. They crashed and slashed their way through the dripping brush, calf-deep in the sticky mud. Nettles and saw-edged grasses lashed the blood from arms and legs, and when the rain stopped at last and the sun came out, swarms of red ants came out to work the mud, and in the process they also worked the toiling, sweating, mud-plastered men. Now and then a *bojong* sounded through the dripping jungle as the unseen scouts paralleled the column and led the way toward the river crossing.

They stopped at the crossing in the late afternoon with the sunlight slanting down through the treetops, raising steam from the soaked earth and jungle. The river was high above the banks, swirling and eddying with tangled vines, logs, and dead animals bobbing up and down on the surface. The guerrillas hauled flimsy-looking log canoes from under the brush and dragged them down to the flood. The patient carabaos stood in the mud while the carts were unloaded and the supplies transferred to the canoes. Trip after trip was made, the paddlers fighting madly to keep the heavily laden canoes from swinging off course or from swamping. One canoe overturned in midriver. Some of the supplies floated down on the current and one of the guerrillas did not rise to the surface.

Bob and Stan were in one of the last canoes to cross, seemingly dragging along some of the swimming carabaos. Bob swung a paddle with the best of them. One of the carabaos bellowed in pain. Bob turned his head. A long, vicious-toothed pair of jaws showed above the swirling muddy current with a great chunk of bleeding meat clamped in it. A Filipino leaned over the side of a canoe, dispatched the mortally wounded carabao with one expert swipe of his bolo, and then cut deeply into the tough hide of the crocodile, which instantly sank out of sight leaving a swirl of bloody foam on the surface of the racing water.

They hauled out the canoes and led the exhausted carabaos up the steep, muddy bank. The sun was almost gone. Already swarms of mosquitoes were rising hungrily to greet the dusk. Frederico Campos wiped the mud from his face. His eyes seemed a little sunken in his head. "The barrio is but a few more miles," he said to Bob and Stan. "There we can have shelter and food. We can get some sleep while the people there watch the trails for the Hapons. Think you can make it?"

Stan slapped a mosquito. "Man, these things got open season on me."

"*Anas*," said Mang Pedro.

Bob looked at him, "*Anas?*"

"Malaria mosquitoes," said Frederico Campos. He slapped at one of them. "We brought in enough atabrine for a couple of months."

"Thank God for that," said Stan.

Campos shook his head. "That was one of the bales that floated down the river."

"Great," murmured Stan.

They slogged on through the dripping jungle in the semi-darkness, their feet sucking and dragging in the mud, with the constant slapping of hands keeping time with their footsteps. Now and then a *bojong* would sound, melancholy and seemingly far away, like a disembodied soul.

4 . . .

THEY COULD SEE the low, flickering fires of the barrio farther up the hill slopes, like rubies cast on black velvet, and the smell of drifting smoke hung in the air, stirred by a shifting and vagrant wind. The guerrillas had stopped in the shelter of the trees beyond a cultivated field. The scouts had gone ahead to contact the villagers.

Bob sat on a log, dead beat, hanging onto the mud-plastered carbine barrel, trying to keep his head up. He had had it. He didn't think he could cross that field to make the barrio, but he knew he'd have to make it under his own power. He looked up at the dried-apple face of Mang Pedro, who had been a young man fifty years ago. Mang Pedro was still erect, although sometimes his heavily veined hands would tremble a little until he clasped them together. Some of the younger guerrillas looked wearier than he did.

Stan Blascovitz lay flat on the ground, his thick chest heaving up and down. "I'm too beat to scratch the bites," he said. He patted Eugene on his little head. "You've got it made, Cousin," he said, "riding the Blascovitz Express all day long."

It was very quiet over at the barrio. The signal to advance would be three calls on a *bojong*, followed by two more, and then three. They certainly were taking their time about it. The smell of cooking food drifted to the hungry, weary men.

The *bojong* sounded three times. The echo had hardly died away when two more calls came, and then three after that, dying softly away on the mountain slopes.

"Come on," said Frederico Campos. He looked at Bob and Stan. "This is the barrio of my good uncle Mang Teodoro, a very old and very wise man. It is called Malitbog. I often stayed here as a child. I have many cousins and second cousins here at Malitbog."

They slogged across the rough field. Sometimes Bob's weary feet struck a hummock that threw him off balance, and he was so beat he would almost fall down. Twice Stan Blascovitz steadied him.

"Maybe Eugene ought to walk," Bob said. "You can carry me instead. Man, that chow smells good."

Stan nodded. He looked intently toward the barrio. "There's something else smelling along with it."

"Pigs. Goats. Dogs," said Bob.

Stan narrowed his eyes. "No," he said. "It reminds me of something else. Something I smelled during the early part of the war." His voice died away.

One of the scouts was waiting at the edge of the field. He looked at Frederico Campos. "It is not good to go in there," he said quietly.

"Why not?" said the officer sharply.

The scout looked away. He fiddled with the bolt handle of his Enfield rifle. "They have been here, sir," he said. "The Hapons . . ."

"Go on!" snapped Campos.

The guerrilla looked miserably at the officer. "You know what they do to barrios suspected of shielding guerrillas, sir."

It was suddenly very quiet. The wind moaned a little

through the trees, and the sound of crackling fire came to the men. They knew now what those fires were, and why it was so quiet in the barrio.

Stan looked at Bob. "I know what that smell is," he said. "We came alongside a burning destroyer on *Grayfin's* first war patrol. Some of the boys were still on it. We got some of them off, but a lot of them died of burns. That smell—" He shook his head.

Frederico Campos slung his rifle over his shoulder. He walked toward the barrio, followed by his men, trailed by Bob and Stan. Here and there huts had been burned to the ground, leaving thick beds of gray ashes from which smoke arose, and as the breeze stirred the ashes, red eyes of fire appeared, like some malevolent creature peering at the intruders from under a gray coverlet, waiting its chance to spring out and destroy. But there had been other destroyers there, and they had done a thorough job of it. Something Ensign Tolliver had told Bob back at Port Darwin came back to him as he walked on the beaten earth of the only street in the barrio. "The guerrilla warfare in the Philippines has developed into a savage give-and-take, with no quarter asked and none given," he had said. Bob knew now what he had meant.

Bodies of villagers were crumpled in the dirt. Some of them were sprawled in the embers of the fires, and the sickeningly sweetish smell once identified would never be forgotten. There were only a few scattered empty brass cartridges lying around. The Japanese liked to work with the bayonet on fighting enemies or on those who were helpless. Some bodies slumped in the lashings that held them to trees, their flesh pierced with many wounds.

"Sometimes, to save ammunition," said a young Filipino quietly, "they herd our people into the houses and nail shut the doors, then fire the buildings. That is what they have done here. That large area of ashes was once the house of Mang Teodoro, the uncle of Lieutenant Campos. A fine old man . . ."

Bob looked at the ashes of the big house. There were odd humped areas, and he knew what they were. The calcined bones of Mang Teodoro, and perhaps the many cousins and second cousins of Frederico Campos.

"There is nothing here save death," said the young Filipino.

A fat raindrop hissed into a bed of ashes. Others plopped on the ground or rattled on the leaves of the trees. The wind stirred the ashes. A flame flickered up eerily, reflecting from the drawn, white faces of the dead. Then the rain slanted down a silvery veil and the acrid smell of wet ashes and hot metal filled the night air.

Frederico Campos looked down at the body of a small child lying sprawled, face upward on the muddy ground. He knelt on one knee and pulled the bloody clothing up over the little face to protect it from the rain. When he stood up, he slung his rifle and set off along the street without a word. One by one his men followed him until only Bob and Stan stood in the street. Stan hitched up his belt and wiped the rain from his broad face. "Come on, kid," he said, "the young Filipino was right."

Bob followed his shipmate. At the edge of the barrio he looked back. There *was* nothing there except death.

Stan looked back at Bob as they slogged along the muddy trail. "Funny thing," he said. "I could have sworn one of the Filipinos said we'd go *north* from the barrio in the morning."

Bob nodded. "He did, Blas."

"We're going south," said the cook.

Lightning flashed across the streaming sky and thunder rolled in the hills. In the brief flash of light Bob saw many tracks in the mud. Most of them were of the bare or sandaled feet of the guerrillas. But there were other tracks. He had seen them before—the tracks of the *tabi*, the split-toed, socklike shoe worn by Japanese troops. There were many of them in the mud, all facing in the same direction in which Frederico Campos was leading his weary, water-soaked men. Bob looked at Stan. Stan picked up something from the ground. It was a Japanese canteen, painted a mustard brown and slung in a webbing harness. Tape had been sewn about part of the webbing, with Japanese characters indicating the owner's name lettered on the tape. Stan whistled softly.

Bob swung his carbine forward and checked it, making sure a cartridge was in the chamber. He slipped on the safety. It looked like a long, wet night march, with the prospect of a hard fight against tough Japanese troops at the end of it.

They stopped in the middle of the night and unloaded the carabaos, caching the precious supplies in the dripping jungle alongside the trail. They turned the carabaos loose. The animals were of no further use, for they could hardly place one hoof ahead of another. That was probably why Lieutenant Campos had changed the direction of the march into the interior. They needed other means of carrying the supplies. There was none to be had in the hills. But the Japanese had transport of one kind or another. Therefore, find the Japanese and strike them, capture *their* transportation, and at the same time take vengeance for the fire and slaughter that had destroyed Malitbog and Mang Teodoro and his people.

The rain had stopped around midnight. Several hours before dawn the exhausted guerrillas and their two allies, the willing but completely worn-out swabbies from the *Grayfin*, dropped to the ground for some sleep. It had turned cold, and a chilly wind blew through the jungle, but Bob slept as though he had been poleaxed. It took Stan Blascovitz a full ten minutes to awaken Bob and he succeeded only by pulling him to his blistered feet and propping him against a tree.

"We're moving out, kid," said Blas. "You want to stay here and wait for us?"

Bob looked dully at him. He couldn't go on and he couldn't stay. "I'll go on," he croaked.

Blas nodded. He came closer to Bob and looked up toward the head of the forming column. "Look, Bob," he said, "we got to stick together. I smell trouble."

"Sure, a bunch of Jap Marines are always trouble," said Bob.

Blas shook his head. "It's not that. It's Campos. He isn't acting right, Bob. I overheard ol' Mang Pedro arguing with him in Tagalog. Sometimes they broke into Spanish, and even English. Ol' Mang Pedro knows a lot more English than he lets on. Well, anyways, the gist of the whole thing is that the old man and a lot of the other Filipinos think Campos is taking too big a risk. We're beat out. We've got only a handful or so of ammo. The Japs are fortified south of here on some barrio beside a river, with barbed wire all around. They've got light and heavy machine guns, mortars, maybe even artillery, and there's likely to be as many of them as there are of us—excepting there might be more of them."

"Campos is doing what he thinks is right. We've got to have transport," said Bob.

Blas took him by the shoulders. "It's not that!" he said fiercely. "Sure we need transport, but not *that* bad! Don't you see Campos is thinking of that barrio back there and all the slaughtered people wiped out like ants! *His* people! Mang Teodoro and Campos' cousins and friends! *That's* what's bugging him, Mac! I think he's gone a little crazy!"

Bob looked toward the line of Filipinos. Tough as they were, they could hardly walk. Blas was right. It was too big a risk. "He ought to pull back," said Bob. "Leave the supplies cached in the jungle and go get transport somewhere else."

"You try and tell him," said Blas dryly.

A *bojong* blew through the darkness. The Filipinos started forward. Campos seemed to have lost his weariness in his hatred of the Japanese and his burning desire to wreak vengeance upon them. They marched for an hour and then waited in the quiet woods while scouts went ahead. Bob and Stan stayed close together. Stan motioned Bob to follow him. They bellied through some brush and stopped at the lip of a steep slope. Below them was a barrio, close to the river, leaden-hued in the darkness. A shielded light showed in one of the buildings. A dog barked.

"Likely loaded to the nines with Hapons," said Blas. He examined his heavy revolver. "Can't quite see myself charging barbed wire with this thing in my hand."

A soft voice spoke behind them. They turned quickly to see the dried-apple face of Mang Pedro. "We do not have the numbers to drink barbed wire," said the old man in passable English. "Is it possible, sirs, that *you* could reason with Lieutenant Campos?"

"We can try," said Blas. He picked up Eugene and followed Mang Pedro through the darkness. Bob looked once more at the dim light down at the barrio. *We do not have the numbers to drink barbed wire,* Mang Pedro had said. Bob suddenly felt cold all over. He quickly followed the two men through the darkness.

The officer was talking with several of his men as the trio approached. He turned to look at them. "Well?" he said in a strange hard voice.

"Mang Pedro says you plan to attack the barrio, sir," said Blas.

"I do."

Blas shrugged. "We're small in numbers, sir. Beat out, as you can see. Very little ammunition."

"We've got to have transport," said Campos shortly.

"Is that the only reason?" said Blas.

"Are you questioning my orders?" said Campos.

"I'm not a guerrilla," said Blas firmly. "I don't have to take orders from you."

"Are you afraid then?"

Bob saw the huge biceps of the cook tighten. Bob swallowed. Campos had said the wrong thing to Stanislaus Blascovitz. "No," said Blas quietly. "I've been on a few war patrols in worse situations than this, but I never served under a skipper that would willingly take a risk like this. You haven't got a chance, sir."

Campos looked at Bob. "And you?" he said.

"I agree with Stan," said Bob, "and with Mang Pedro."

Campos turned quickly to look at the old man. The officer's hand hovered over the butt of his automatic pistol. "So," he said coldly, "you've turned against me, Mang Pedro."

The old man was not afraid. "Do not try to look into the face of death too long, sir, else it will take you. This is madness, sir."

Campos bit his lip. He looked around at the others. "Will you also disobey me?" he asked.

There was no answer. Campos drew his pistol and waved it. "Come!" he said. "They are all asleep. We can be through the wire before they are alerted. We need those trucks they have!" He strode down the hill.

One by one the men shrugged. Singly, and then by twos and threes they walked after him until only Mang Pedro and the two Americans stood there. Mang Pedro unslung his Enfield rifle and walked after the others. Blas looked at Bob. "Stay close. We'll follow them. If it looks bad, head for the tall timber, kid. This is none of our fight—at least the way *he's* going about it."

They stopped at the bottom of the hill in the thick brush. Beyond them was the road, with barbed wire entanglements filling the areas between the barrio and the road. It was very quiet. The dog had stopped barking. One of the scouts must have slipped in and killed him.

Bob checked his carbine again, and as he raised his head he began to count the men. There had been at least seventy-five of them up on the hill, but there couldn't be more than fifty standing at the bottom of the hill. Even as Bob watched he saw two more men fade silently into the brush. Only Lieutenant Campos stepped out on the road. More men faded away. They had no heart for this sort of thing, nor could they be blamed for pulling foot. They were *buqweeing* as fast as they could.

Bob opened his mouth to tell Blas. Blas quickly shook his head. "I don't like the smell of this, Bob," he said tensely.

Campos raised his left hand and cut it sharply toward the wire. He did not look back as he trotted forward. Only one man stood in the road watching him. It was Mang Pedro. Campos reached the far side of the road. He reached out a hand toward the wire. Instantly a floodlight was turned on, making the lean handsome officer's face into a bluish mask. The whole area, including the road, was bathed in light. Campos yelled once and tried to get through the wire. A machine gun rattled fiercely, spitting orange-red flames. Campos' body jerked. He fell over the wire.

"Let's get out of here!" said Stan.

Mang Pedro raised his rifle. He fired once at the

machine gun. It stopped chattering. The old man charged forward as he had in the old days, fighting against Aguinaldo and his rebels. He shouted fiercely as he ran toward the officer. The machine gun chattered again. Mang Pedro spun about and went down on his knees in the middle of the road. His head shook. He looked toward his fallen officer, and then his body heaved convulsively. Blood, looking jet-black in the ghastly light, poured from his slack mouth, and he pitched forward on his face to lie still.

"Come on!" yelled Stan. "They'll be right after us!"

Bob shook his head. He raised his carbine and aimed at the floodlight. He emptied half of the magazine into it, and the glass shattered. The light dimmed, turned orange, deepened into red, then ruby red, and then was out completely. The rest of the carbine magazine was emptied toward the chattering machine gun. There was a short pause in its operation, but it started in again, backed by two more. Somewhere in the darkness a mortar coughed, and the shell burst in the woods. A Filipino screamed like a wounded animal.

Bob ran after Stan. All his weariness seemed to vanish as he slogged on after the cook, the brush tearing at his body and branches whipping across his face. A truck engine roared into life and another and another. The eastern sky was faintly graying; it was the dawn. By sunup the trails, roads, and the adjoining jungle would be thick with Hapons thirsting for guerrilla blood.

5 . . .

EVERY HALF HOUR the Kalow birds would start in: *Kalow . . . kalow . . . kalow . . .* First one would start to set the key and the others would join in, one after the other, with a deep, rumbling sound that would roll across the hills toward the coastline for about fifteen seconds. Suddenly they would stop altogether. They sounded just like a cuckoo clock, but deeper. Every half hour, almost to the second, they'd start in again. In the intervals the white cockatoos would shriek madly, like an insane chorus, backed by the chattering of the little monkeys. The *bojongs* mixed in with the outlandish symphony, but this time it was the *bojong* birds who were sounding off, *not* the guerrilla scouts.

Bob lay belly flat on the edge of a steep slope, peering down toward the stream that was hardly visible because of the thick growths. Stan had gone down for water half an hour earlier. Bob looked back at young Zapanta, the only one left of all the guerrillas who had *buqweed* off before Frederico Campos had singlehandedly attacked the Japanese barrio.

"You think he's all right, Zapanta?" he asked anxiously.

Zapanta smiled through the mask of dried mud on his thin face. "Who can harm *that* one? Besides, does he not have his cousin Eugene with him? What harm can come to the big one as long as he has Eugene to take care of him?"

Bob grinned in spite of his fears. They had been fleeing through the foothills for three days. All the others had vanished. Now and then they had heard the quick, staccato sound of automatic weapons firing, echoing through the jungle and rebounding from the hills, and then it had been very silent for a time until the birds and monkeys had started in again. He looked down at his muddy, rust-flecked carbine. He had only five rounds of ammunition left for it. Zapanta still carried his 1917 Enfield rifle, but, in common with most Enfields, the weak extractor had broken, and unless Zapanta could pry out the empty shell casing, his weapon was useless except as a club.

Bob looked back over his shoulder. "How much farther?" he said.

"Twenty miles at least."

Bob rested his head on the ground. Sweat soaked through his filthy shirt and ran down his sides. He could feel the ants crawling up his legs. He was too tired to care. His head snapped up, however, when the sound of a single shot echoed through the jungle along the stream, instantly silencing the birds and the monkeys. There was a crashing in the brush and Stan appeared, running clumsily, with Eugene hanging onto his neck for dear life. The cook waved his smoking pistol. "A scout," he said hoarsely. "Nearly walked right on top of me. I got him a second before he got me with his bayonet. Look!" He pointed to his side. His dirty undershirt was stained with a growing patch of blood. "Sliced right past my ribs!" Stan dashed the sweat from his face. "We've got to keep on!"

Bob looked wearily up at him. It was hopeless. Three

times in three days they had just managed to squeak past Japanese patrols or men of the BC—the Bureau of Constabulary formed of Filipinos by the Japanese—in their grayish-purple uniforms of short pants and short-sleeved shirts. The roads and trails seemed alive with Hapons and BC's.

"Come on, Bob!" said Stan.

"Wait!" said Zapanta. He was looking into the jungle behind them.

"They *behind* us too?" asked Stan. He cocked his revolver.

"Wait! Quiet!" whispered the Filipino.

Bob rolled over and sat up, looking into the tangled greenery of the jungle. A chilling feeling of fear crept over him despite the sluggish heat of the day. There was something in there. He didn't know *what* it was; *but there was something in there.* He raised his carbine.

"No!" snapped Zapanta.

Then Bob saw *something* or *somebody* watching him from behind a tree, only to vanish so quickly he wasn't even sure he had seen anything or anybody. A soft trilling birdcall sounded. Minutes ticked past.

"We can't sit around here looking for will-o'-the-wisps, Zapanta," growled Stan.

"Quiet!" ordered Zapanta again. He looked over his shoulder at Stan. "Those will-o'-the wisps might just get us out of this mess, Blas. Take it easy!"

Bob looked back down the trail. If there had been one Japanese down there, there would be others. He turned his head again and saw a face, framed between leaf fronds, not ten feet from him. A little dark face, with intensely bright eyes, and a head topped by a mass of fuzzy hair. Bob thought for a moment that it might be a large monkey, but then the face smiled. The trilling birdcall came from the pursed lips.

56

"Thank God!" said Zapanta. "They are Mangyan people!" He looked at Bob. "They are our friends. They hate the Japanese. Look!"

A man almost totally naked except for a breechclout had stepped out of the jungle. He was about four feet high, but his bushy hair made him look taller. He was perfectly formed, a miniature man, with well-shaped muscles. He had a tiny bow in his left hand.

Zapanta pointed down the hill. "Hapons!" he said earnestly.

The little man nodded and said something in his native tongue. He pointed into the jungle to one side of the trail. Then he turned and vanished as quickly as he had appeared.

"Come on!" said Zapanta. "*Sigi legi, ho!*" He plunged into the jungle. Bob and Stan wasted no time in following him. They could just make out the frizzy head of the little man as he led them through the seemingly trackless jungle. They went up a steep slope, and all of a sudden there were more of the Mangyan to be seen, busily working in the tall, saw-edged grass along the trail that the three men had been following.

"*Oi* there! *Oi!*" called out a man.

They looked as a tall American carrying an automatic rifle stepped out of the brush. Twin-holstered issue Colts hung at either hip, and a heavy sheath knife was slantwise across his middle. A Filipino hat woven of leaves was on his head, and he wore faded suntans. "Get in here," he said curtly. "Keep quiet. You're all right now. Jump!"

They scuttled into the brush. The man placed a hand to his mouth and blew through it, exactly like the trilling birdcall the Mangyan had made. The little people working alongside the trail in the grass scampered up the slope, laughing among themselves, only to disappear into the thick undergrowth. The jungle was very quiet now. No sound of birds or monkeys. Someone was down along the slopes leading toward the higher area where the trail cut between the low, forested hills.

The American looked back at the three men who were watching him. "I'm Jim Bledsoe," he said. "Commander of this area. I'm a little short of boys, but I think we can make out all right. Can you use those guns?"

"Extractor broken," said Zapanta.

"Five rounds left," said Stan.

"Five rounds here," said Bob.

Bledsoe nodded. "We'll arm you later. Use what you have. But don't open fire until I do! Understand?" He unsheathed a Colt automatic and handed it to Zapanta.

They watched the trail. A Japanese appeared, walking softly in his tabied feet, a bayoneted Arisaka rifle swinging back and forth as he scanned the trail through his eyeglasses. He waved someone on and walked up the trail, right below the watching people on the higher slopes. A moment later two more Japanese soldiers appeared, walking slowly, poking into the grass with long glittering bayonets. The two soldiers moved on. The sound of a cricket came from one of them. He looked back down the trail. The head of a column of Japanese soldiers appeared. There were at least fifty of them, with some hauling light carts carrying machine guns. An officer led the way, a cloth flapping at the back of his head to protect the nape of his neck from the sun. A long samurai sword hung at his side.

The column was fairly in the center of the trail now. Bledsoe slid his BAR forward and looked back at the others. He winked. The BAR stuttered into life. Instantly the Japanese leaped to lie flat in the tall grass. The instant they hit the ground they shrieked, screamed, and cursed. Some of them jumped to their feet, gripping bloody spots on their uniforms. Their eyes were wide in their sweaty faces.

"Now, now!" yelled Bledsoe.

Bob fired until his carbine ran dry. Japanese were running wildly in every direction, while others rolled over and over in the saw-edged grass, gripping their bodies and screaming at the top of their lungs. A few of them managed to open fire but there was no direction to it. All they could see was the jerking muzzle of the heavy Browning automatic rifle spitting flame and death at them. The BAR ran dry; Bledsoe jerked out the empty magazine and slammed another into place. The twenty rounds of .30/06 ripped into the milling Japanese, scattering them like tenpins. The Japanese broke, fleeing down the road in utter disorder, leaving their machine-gun carts in the road. The officer shrieked and cursed, swinging his glittering samurai blade over his head. Some of the soldiers began to rally. Stan Blascovitz thrust forward his heavy revolver and rested it on a log. He fired three times, and the officer spun about and fell, his sword clattering on the trail. The rally broke with the death of the officer.

The firing stopped. Smoke drifted down the trail. Here and there wounded Japanese moaned and cried out. There were many dead. Bledsoe reloaded his BAR. He stood up. "Don't go near the wounded," he said. "They won't surrender and they'll try to take you with them if they get a chance."

"What about the scouts up the trail?" said Stan.

Bledsoe wiped the sweat from his lean face. "They won't be back," he said cryptically.

Bob looked up the jungle trail to where the scouts had gone. It was very quiet. He suddenly realized that the little Mangyan men had also vanished into that brooding jungle. He knew now why the scouts would not be back.

"What about the wounded?" said Stan.

Bledsoe looked at him. "You know what they do to *our* wounded?" he asked quietly.

"I've seen some of their work already," said Stan.

Bledsoe nodded. "They *play* with ours, mister. Bayonet practice and other amusements."

"Just because they do it," said Bob, "is no reason why *we* have to do it."

"Hear! Hear!" jeered Bledsoe. His face changed into a hard mask. "Listen, kid! This is *guerrilla* warfare. The first time you see their saltwater treatment you'll lose some of that high-falutin mercy and honor."

"Saltwater treatment?" said Blas curiously.

"One of their favorite treatments for a captured prisoner. They tie his hands and feet and run a cord around his neck, so that if he struggles, he strangles himself. They wedge open his mouth and hold his nose closed. They pour seawater into his open mouth, and I mean lots of it! He has to swallow to breathe. He gets all the sensations of drowning and when his abdomen is extended with the water they *jump* on it!"

Bob swallowed hard as he thought of all that seawater. He had almost drowned once. He knew what Bledsoe meant. "All the same, *we* aren't animals, Bledsoe."

Bledsoe laughed. He checked his automatic rifle and his pistol and walked down the slope, digging in his bootheels.

Young Zapanta looked at Bob. "He is right, you know." He followed Bledsoe down the hill. They saw him get a loaded pistol clip from Bledsoe. He slid it into the butt of the heavy .45 caliber pistol and looked up at the two sailors. Stan turned on a heel and walked into the dimness of the jungle with Eugene strangely silent on his back. Bob started after Stan. The first pistol report cracked flatly and echoed along the trail. In the next five minutes there were ten more of them and then it was very quiet.

They heard Bledsoe whistle sharply. Stan shrugged. "Might as well face it," he said.

They slid down the grassy slope and walked past the dead, who stared up at the hot sun with eyes that did not see. Zapanta was piling Arisaka rifles in the center of the trail, along with a few Nambu automatic pistols. "Gather the grenades," he said to the two *Grayfin* men. "We use anything we can get."

"Watch the grass!" snapped Bledsoe. "Here, you!" he snarled at Zapanta. "You would have let them walk into the *bagakay!*"

"*Bagakay?*" said Bob stupidly.

Bledsoe nodded. He picked up a Japanese rifle and parted the saw-edged grass. "Look," he said. The ground was studded with slender, wet-looking double-barbed pieces of bamboo. Some of them were red with Japanese blood. "These are *suak,*" said the guerrilla. "Made out of *bagakay* bamboo shoots. They are poisonous. We make mine fields, Filipino style, out of them. There are hundreds of them in the grass on either side of the trail. We plan an ambush this way. Let the Nips get right in among them, then unexpectedly open fire. Natural reaction is to hit for cover, as you saw them do. When they light, they ram these *suak* into their bodies. They aren't about to be very efficient in returning our fire with these babies needling into them, so we have time enough to smash them up, as you saw."

"If they're poisonous," said Bob quietly, "why do you have to shoot at them at all?"

Bledsoe spat to one side. "It isn't that deadly, but it does fester. Those Nips that took off will find that out by tomorrow."

Bob looked away from the hard face of the guerrilla. Somehow he didn't mind the Mangyan, or native Filipinos fighting this way, but it didn't seem natural for an *American* to do so.

Stan hitched Eugene higher on his shoulder. He looked sideways at Bob. "They don't give or ask quarter in this Bamboo War, kid," he said.

The Mangyan people came out of the jungle, laughing and chattering, oddly reminding Bob of the monkeys that hung quietly in the treetops, waiting for the intruders to leave, and yet these little men showed quick intelligence in their eyes and expressions. Swiftly they set to work piling the Japanese equipment into the machine-gun carts that had been left behind. Some of them had gone on down the trail to watch for the possible return of the enemy.

The trilling birdcall sounded three times. But by that time the Mangyan had disappeared up the trail into the thick cover of the jungle, hauling the heavily laden carts with them. Bledsoe shoved back his hat and wiped the sweat from his face. "You want to stay and have a service for the dead?" he said sarcastically.

Bob shoved a Nambu pistol into his belt and picked up an Arisaka rifle he had appropriated until such time as he could get more cartridges for his carbine. "You've got a great sense of humor, Mister," he said.

Bledsoe looked down the trail. "The Nips are on the way back," he said. "Likely got the rest of their boys coming on the double. We'd better *sigi legi, ho!*"

Stan had slung a Japanese automatic rifle over his shoulder. He picked up some loaded magazines and started up the trail, followed by Bob. Zapanta glanced at Bob and hurried on ahead. Bledsoe picked up the glittering samurai saber and waved it. "Banzai!" he said. He laughed. "You want this for a souvenir?"

62

Bob did not answer or look around. He heard the saber drop to the ground. A moment later Bledsoe was striding easily alongside him, his heavy BAR slung over a broad shoulder. "Listen, kid," he said quietly. "I wasn't this way when the war started. I was on the Bataan Death March and only managed to escape by the grace of God. We've been fighting a war on not much else than sheer nerve in these islands ever since. I'm not making excuses. It's the way we fight here. No quarter asked or given. It's as simple as that. This the first time you've seen any action?"

"I've been around," said Bob quietly.

"You were pretty good with that carbine," said the guerrilla.

Bob looked sideways at him and smiled. "You're pretty handy with the BAR, Mister."

"*¡Gracias!* It's my stock-in-trade. By the way, the boys all call me Jungle Jim, on account of my two automatics."

"Very fitting," said Bob.

They walked into the dimness of the jungle. "We'll hole up at the Mangyan village for a little while," said Bledsoe. "We were expecting those supplies you brought in on *Grayfin* and we couldn't afford to have that *boroba* break up back there when Fred Campos got killed. We needed every man in that force. That's why I had to use the Mangyan. Lucky for us they're on our side."

"I've never seen anything like them," said Bob.

Bledsoe nodded. "You might call them a tiny remnant of prehistoric man. There are about eleven thousand of them here on Mindoro, and we could hardly exist without their help. The ethnologists identify them as 'a primitive, pygmy people, unassimilated descendants of prehistoric immigrants from the Pacific and Indian Ocean Islands and the mainland of Asia.' I suppose that's about as good an evaluation as you could make of them. When we established our guerrilla base not far from their country, we

63

never saw them, although we knew they were watching us all the time. The Director of Non-Christian Tribes on Mindoro Island talked with them, telling them we would make them welcome. Four of their leaders came to us with gifts to make sure they were welcome. After that they came in companies. They are completely oblivious to the value of money, which is one thing you can say is an advantage over more 'civilized' peoples. That's the reason why the Nips couldn't buy them off as they did many Filipinos. It makes little difference to the Mangyan who is in power, since their lives are lived out in and around their hidden villages. Even so, they don't like the Japanese."

"That was obvious enough," said Bob dryly. "By the way, how did you know we came from *Grayfin* and about Lieutenant Campos' getting killed?"

Bledsoe tapped the side of his head. "Bamboo Telegraph," he said mysteriously. He lighted a cigar. "Wait a minute," he added. He walked over to the side of the trail and dropped behind a log, thrusting his heavy weapon atop it. Bob walked behind him and squatted in the brush. He looked curiously at Bledsoe. The guerrilla was calmly blowing smoke rings. He thrust a finger through one of the rings and grinned at Bob. Bob couldn't help grinning back.

The birds were calling and the monkeys were chattering, evidently oblivious to the two men beside the trail. Suddenly they stopped. Bledsoe nodded. He sighted down the trail. A minute or two ticked past, and all at once the heavy weapon crashed into noisy, chattering life, sweeping twenty rounds down the trail. A man screamed. A rifle cracked. Something whipped through the leaves over Bob's head.

Bledsoe calmly took out the empty magazine and slid

64

it into his canvas magazine pouch, replacing it with a fully loaded clip. "Last magazine in the locker," he said. "Well, that will hold them up long enough for us to get far enough ahead of them to escape. They won't follow us too quickly."

They walked up the trail leaving the acrid odor of burned powder behind them. In a little while the monkeys started chattering. Cockatoos screamed raucously. Then came the lone sound of a Kalow bird starting the pitch, followed by the steady rumbling chorus of the others. Their ancestors had been doing just that, long before man had appeared on Mindoro, and they would probably be doing it long after man had disappeared from Mindoro.

6 . . .

T HEY HAD CLIMBED higher and higher into the hills all
that long, hot day, and when dusk came, they were
still climbing. By seven o'clock that night Bob was ready
to drop, but just about that time he was aware of the
faint flickering light of a fire somewhere higher up the
slopes and the faintest suggestion of moonlight in the
eastern sky. One thing he had noticed, despite his weariness, was that they seemed to have left the mosquitoes
far below. Here the brush had been cleared away, and
they walked through an area that was almost park-
like.

"What about the Japs?" asked Stan. "Won't they see
those fires?"

Bledsoe shook his head. "Not from below. If these
people hear a plane they douse the fires. They can hear
a plane coming minutes before we can. Besides, the Japs
don't like to bomb their villages unless they absolutely
have to, because they think this will all be part of the
Greater East Asia Co-Prosperity Sphere, and they know
they'll eventually have to make friends with these little
people. Seems crazy that a powerful, modern nation of
millions, a first-class power in the world, has to worry
about making friends with about eleven thousand, four-

foot-high, primitive people like the Mangyan, but I suppose the Nips *want* to be loved."

The moon had topped the eastern side of the mountains by the time the weary quartet reached the village. It shed a silvery light over hills seemingly frosted with clouds. The air was sweet and cool. The leaves of the trees shone in the clear moonlight.

The Mangyans lived in tree houses on bamboo platforms about thirty-five feet from the ground. The houses were neatly thatched with grass. Knotted ropes hung down from the houses, and even as Bob watched he saw a little man swiftly climb the rope, using his hands and big toes to go up the knots.

The smell of woodsmoke and cooking food hung in the windless air. A Mangyan came to Bledsoe and spoke swiftly to him, with many gestures of his tiny hands. Bledsoe nodded. "He says they have made a house for their guests. Come and rest in it and food will be brought."

"Very nice of the little fellow," said Stan. "I'm beginning to like these friendly little guys."

Bob nodded, and then he remembered those deadly sprigs of barbed *bagakay* hidden by the hundreds in the grass along the trail, so deadly and unseen. He shivered a little. He was glad they were friendly to the guerrillas rather than to the Japanese.

They had made a neat house of bamboo, thatched with grass, set a foot or so off the ground. Strips of white bamboo flooring were separated a quarter of an inch or so both for ventilation and to sweep the dust and debris through to the ground beneath. A box of sand served as a stove and an iron tripod hung over it. A rack had been built over the stove upon which to dry green wood for the fire. Mats were neatly rolled up in a corner, and there were water jugs in another corner.

The Mangyan who had led them proudly to their newly built quarters lighted a lamp made of a long green leaf wrapped around a chunk of gutta-percha. It cast a soft, yellowish light.

"Neat, hey?" said Bledsoe. He stripped off his magazine webbing and leaned his BAR in a corner. He dropped onto the floor and unlaced his jungle boots. "Make yourselves comfy, boys. We'll be here a few days at least. Don't worry about the Nips. The Mangyan will spot them miles from here."

"Where do we go from here, Jim?" asked Bob wearily.

"Over to the main base. About three days' marching."

"Great," murmured Bob. He peeled off what remained of his shoes. A sole hung from one of them, and the other had only half a heel. Inside, he could see blackish bloodstains from his raw feet. He began to peel off the improvised bandages he had wound about his ruined feet. His many insect bites itched intolerably.

"Hey! Look!" said Stan from the doorway.

Bob crawled over beside the big cook. Far, far below them through a great notch in the hills, the moon was shining on a vast expanse of water, turned silvery by the moonlight.

"The South China Sea," said Jim Bledsoe behind them. "Beautiful, isn't it?"

"It would look better with a Yank task force plowing it up," said Stan.

Bledsoe leaned against the side of the doorway. "There will be, before the year is out," he said.

"You're kidding!" said Bob.

Bledsoe shook his head. "We received orders from MacArthur to set up weather stations all through these islands. They say they've even got radio stations set up in the Gobi Desert to relay weather information back to headquarters in Australia, but don't ask me why."

Bob looked up. "Maybe for planes to bomb Japan. They'd have to have information at least twenty-four hours ahead of time. I heard some talk about it back at Port Darwin."

"Scuttlebutt," said Stan.

Bledsoe lighted a twisted cigar and drew in a lungful of smoke. "Another thing—we've got to plot channels through the minefields in Surigao Straits between Homonhon off southern Samar and southern Leyte.

"Great," said Bob. "That's a *little* distance from Mindoro, isn't it?"

Bledsoe nodded. He blew out a cloud of smoke. "About three hundred miles, I'd say."

"How do you propose going about it?" asked Bob.

Bledsoe shrugged. "There isn't much guerrilla organization around there. We've got the best radio setup, such as it is. Ours not to reason why, lads."

"Anything else?" asked Stan.

Bledsoe nodded. "We're to establish coast watcher stations and mobile radio stations along Verde Island Passage, just north of this island. It's a vital east-west link between San Bernardino Strait and the South China Sea. A natural sea-lane from the Pacific to the Orient. Trouble is the Japs are thick as fleas out there. Plane, submarine, and surface-craft patrols. Garrisons of Jap Marines on the islands. Big gun batteries on Verde Island. It won't be easy. We sure needed those radios you lads lost back there. If Fred Campos hadn't tried to make a hero out of himself, we would have had them by now." Bledsoe shook his head. "Well, we'll do the best we can. Here comes the chow!"

Several of the little men brought a steaming iron pot to the shack and placed it on the floor. Gravely they handed each of their guests broad, thick leaves for plates, thrust a big wooden ladle into the steaming mess of food, and then they vanished, but Bob had the feeling they were watching from somewhere outside. It was downright uncanny how they could see and still be unseen.

Bledsoe ladled out the chow. Bob sniffed at it. He nodded in satisfaction. It smelled delicious. Some kind of meat mixed with vegetables and shoots. "Mangyan chop suey," he said.

They ate voraciously. Bledsoe kept dipping more of the food from the pot. It didn't seem to have a bottom. Stan Blascovitz nodded in satisfaction. "Terrific," he said. He held out some of the food to Eugene. "Here you are, Cousin."

It was the first time Bob had ever seen the little monkey refuse food. Eugene made queer squealing noises and turned his head away. "Wonder what's bugging him?" said Stan curiously.

Bledsoe shrugged. He dumped a full ladle on Stan's leaf. "Eat hearty, Blas. There's more where this came from."

Stan poked about in the food and came up with some dark-looking meat which still clung to some tiny bones. He gnawed at the meat with the grease running down his chin. Then slowly his jaws stopped moving. He held the piece of meat and bone toward the guttering lamp. It was a tiny hand, like that of a child.

Stan looked at Bledsoe with wide eyes. "What is this, Jim?" he said in a hoarse voice.

Bledsoe swallowed and picked a stringy piece of meat from between his even white teeth with a fingernail. "Monkey stew, Blas. Good, isn't it?"

Stan bolted for the door, with Eugene shrieking after him. Bob felt his stomach rise a little and roll over, and a sour taste came into the base of his throat. He felt the eyes of the other two on him, and he knew *he* wasn't going to get sick, not in front of them at least. "Delicious," he murmured. Cold sweat beaded his face.

"More?" said Bledsoe politely. He lifted the ladle.

Bob shook his head. "I've made a pig out of myself already." He smiled weakly. "You'd have thought Blas had eaten some of his own cooking."

Bledsoe slapped a hand on his thigh. "Pretty good! Pretty good! We'll make a real Bamboo Warrior out of you yet, kid."

"I can hardly wait," Bob said.

"Cannibals!" roared Blas from outside.

Bob had to join in the laughter. It was the first time he had ever seen Blas really discomfited by something, for the big cook had always taken everything else in the war in stride.

Jim Bledsoe worked on Bob's feet after chow. He soaked off the blood-crusted bandages and made Bob sit for at least an hour with his feet in water as hot as he could stand. Then he swabbed the feet with a salve he got from one of the little men, and rebandaged the feet.

"You're pretty good at that," said Bob admiringly. "You must have been in the Medics."

Jim shook his head. "Infantry. You have to look out for the men's feet. That's your first consideration. Take care of their feet and teach them how to shoot. That's all they have to know."

Bob leaned back against the matting. "You must have been a noncom. Corporal? Sergeant?"

Bledsoe shook his head. "Nothing like that."

"Not a Pfc.!" said Bob in delight. "I've got rank on you if you were."

Bledsoe stood up and yawned. "Battalion commander," he said.

Zapanta rubbed his thin face. He looked sideways at

Bob. "Lieutenant-Colonel James Bledsoe," he said casually. "United States Army, assigned as instructor to the Philippine Army."

Bob stared.

"West Point, Class of 1923," said Zapanta relentlessly. "Honor man of his class. Decorated with the Distinguished Service Cross for action on Leyte by Douglas MacArthur himself before MacArthur left for Australia."

Bledsoe felt for a cigar. "You can close your mouth now, Bob," he said. He picked up the guttering lamp, knocked the crusted carbon from it, and lighted his cigar. "I'll take a look at Blas. Maybe he feels like a bedtime snack or something." He left the shack, contentedly puffing at his cigar.

Bob closed a fist. "I ought to belt you a good one, Zapanta," he said coldly. "You knew that all the time. What's the big idea? Come on! Tell me before I work you over."

Zapanta grinned. "You hit me, kid, and I'll have you up for a drumhead court-martial. *You*, sir, are addressing First Lieutenant Zapanta Morelos, Class of 1940, Philippine Military Academy."

Bob stared again.

"You can close your mouth now, Bob," said Zapanta.

"Beats me," said Bob wearily. "This is the craziest part of the war I've been in yet, and I haven't missed much of the sideshows, so to speak."

Zapanta made a few mystical passes in the air with his hands. "Like the man says: 'You ain't seen nothin' yet!'"

Later, as Bob lay on his mats, looking through the doorway down to the far-distant South China Sea, he began to wonder about *Grayfin*. Maybe the Bamboo Telegraph would know what had happened to the submarine—and Gary, of course. He wondered how Gary would have reacted to eating monkey meat. Gary would eat a chunk out of anything seemingly edible. There were radios on Mindoro, as Colonel Bledsoe had said, but *Grayfin* would be unlikely to break radio silence if she *had* escaped.

"Kid?" said Blas from his mats.

"Yeh?" said Bob.

"I got a feeling we're going to stay with these boys for quite a while. It isn't likely we can get back on *Grayfin,* even if she did escape. Right?"

"Right," agreed Bob sleepily.

Blas shifted and moved the sleeping Eugene a little. "Bledsoe thinks there'll be a task force in these waters sometime later this year. Man, I want to be on a ship or a sub when *that* happens. How about you?"

"Yes," said Bob. He rolled over and looked at Blas. "Fat chance, though," he said.

"This a rough war in these islands," said the cook soberly.

"It's rough everywhere," said Bob.

Blas nodded. "Still, I can't help thinking about all those Filipino boys and some of ours getting shot up at the beach. And Campos dying on that wire."

"I was thinking of Mang Pedro," said Bob.

"Yeh," said Blas quietly, "but he was a *soldier.* Maybe he wanted it that way. Better for a man to die on his feet facing the enemy in his country than to die in bed with a lot of memories no one else knows anything about. They won't ever forget Mang Pedro now. He was a *man,* kid."

The owls hooted softly in the trees as Bob drifted off to sleep. He, too, could still see the old Philippine Scout, alone of all the *boroba,* stepping out into that floodlighted road, carrying his many years like a young man . . . a Philippine Scout who had been a friend to the father of General Douglas MacArthur. With such men, it was certainly possible to free the Philippines from the Japanese clutches, but it would require the help of the United States. When would that time come? "I shall return," Douglas MacArthur had said. He was not a man who did not keep a promise.

7 . . .

THE BAMBOO TELEGRAPH had sped its message from the coast, through the deep jungles and rugged foothills, to the mountain slopes where the Mangyan people played hosts to Colonel Jim Bledsoe, Lieutenant Zapanta Morelos, Stan Blascovitz, and Bob Dunbar. It was mostly good news of one sort, and some bad news of another. *Grayfin* had been badly hurt, but had managed to escape and was on her way back to Australia. There was no record of crew casualties. The Japanese had left the coastal area where they had attacked *Grayfin* and were regrouping farther south, but they were still in great strength and were getting reinforcements in daily by ship from Luzon. Air activity was heavier than usual over Verde Island Passage. But the way was clear to reach the guerrilla base to the north. The bad news was that virtually none of the supplies brought in by *Grayfin* had been saved. That which had not been destroyed on the beach, or carried off by the submarine, had been captured by the Japanese, including the cached supplies left behind by Campos in his abortive sortie on the Japanese-held barrio. The few supplies that had been salvaged were not of great value. Worst of all, the new and powerful radios, as well as all the weather-station gear that was so vital for preinvasion plans, had been lost.

Jim Bledsoe had not taken the loss of the new radios and the vital weather-station gear too badly. "Well," he had said, "there's no use crying about it, lads. We'll have to makee-do as we always have done with what we have. There isn't much time left though. The sooner we get out of here and to the temporary base the sooner we can get the ball rolling. Seems as though the Japs have managed to find a way to spot our supply subs as they did *Grayfin,* and until we can figure out *how* they're doing it, we'll have to fight this war in the old-fashioned way."

They had left the hospitable Mangyan people, and guided by several of the little men, they threaded their way through the rugged hills to the northwest. Ominously enough, they saw many Japanese float-type reconnaissance planes skimming low over the hills, many more than Bledsoe had ever seen before.

The temporary base was not far from the coast in an old barrio that had been abandoned long before the war and virtually forgotten until necessity had brought it back to life. The Japanese didn't know it was there, and it was almost impossible for their recon planes to spot. In its liveliest days it had been a drowsy, thatched-up and tinned-over collection of shacks, dusty, fusty, and rusty, and time had not been kind to it. The old church still stood, thick-walled and defiant, with a small galvanized shed beside it in which hung three church bells as well as the big iron hammer used for striking them. Some of the shacks stood on stilts, with chickens scratching and clucking beneath them. "Snake guards," explained Zapanta to Bob and Blas. "Snakes like houses because they are cool by day and warm by night, but when they head for the houses, they get sidetracked by going after the chickens. The chickens squawk and warn the people in the houses. Very simple. *¿No es verdad?*"

The dry wind rattled the leaves of the coconut palms and swept the heat away. It was very pleasant on the great hill slope with the South China Sea sparkling in the bright sunlight, with dark-green jungle-matted islands here and there. Zapanta pointed out several of them. "They have Hapon Marines on them, and some big guns at least 75mm. They run patrol boats through the passages. Subchasers armed with machine guns and 75mm. guns. I personally haven't seen any of their submarines out there, but some of the others have, and of course there is always their air patrol. See! There is one of them now!"

Far below the sun flashed on the wings of a plane that was slowly wheeling about at a low altitude, probably examining something at close range.

"There is nothing to fear here," said the Filipino. "We are safe from them, except if the Kalibapi get in their dirty work." He spat to one side. "They are filthy Filipinos who masquerade under political societies, enlisting local citizens as spies to serve out here in the field. They are hard to spot, my friends. But, when we do catch one . . ." His voice trailed off.

Bob looked quickly at him. The Filipino's normally pleasant face was a mask of intense hatred. He had not even looked like that when he was killing the Japanese.

The sound of metal pounding against metal drifted about the sleepy-looking barrio. Files rasped and hacksaws whined through metal. There was a smell of dust, explosives, metal filings, gasoline, and oil about the place, and yet no one was seen on the streets. The four new arrivals had been passed on several times by guard posts farther down the slopes, and they knew they were being watched by some of the Mangyan who were from a village other than the one at which they had stayed.

Bob peered into some of the small open-sided bodegas,

77

or warehouses, that stood under the tall trees. Thatching covered the roof of the buildings, blending in with the living thatch of the trees that provided shade for the barrio. There were long, crude workbenches set up inside the bodegas, at which sat many Filipinos hard at work.

"Making .30/06 bullets," said Zapanta. "It is too bad we lost all those cartridges from your submarine, but these will still do."

Bob saw a pile of brass rods from which pieces about the length of a .30/06 bullet were being cut. Others were filing one end into the ovoid shape of the bullet point. A small Filipino had set up an old Springfield rifle in a vise and was ramming one of the newly filed cartridges through it with a bamboo ramrod to try it for fit.

"Those rods look like curtain rods," said Blas.

Zapanta nodded. "They *are* curtain rods. By a stroke of sheer fortune we found out that most of the schoolhouses had been providentially furnished with such beautiful brass curtain rods. They are a little thicker than .30 caliber, but they are cut to length, filed to a point, then filed to fit, driven through that old rifle to make *sure* they fit, and then are ready for their casing and charges."

"They make those out of something from the school-houses?" asked Stan.

Jim Bledsoe shook his head. "We use old cartridge cases. Some of them are pretty badly beat up and paper thin, but it's the best we can do. Primers are made out of sulphur mixed with coconut-shell carbon and a little antimony. I'd say they have about 89 to 90 percent efficiency. We got some powder out of Jap sea mines, but the stuff was too powerful, so we added pulverized wood to retard the burning. The mine powder blew up a slew of rifles, firing pins, extractors, and rifle bolts before we got the right combination. We measured the powder by guess

78

in the early days until we got some accurate measuring funnels and things from a sub."

Zapanta grinned. "Well, anyway, you don't require windage when you fire off one of those babies, fellows. I've burned my hands many a time with powder flashes between the bolts."

Bledsoe nodded. "Especially the 1917 Enfields. Blew out a lot of them. They always had weak extractors anyway. We had to make more of them out of spring steel. Lasted for about a dozen rounds as a rule."

Bob looked at the industrious Filipinos. "How many rounds can they make in a day, sir?" he asked Bledsoe.

"Sixty men can average about one hundred and sixty rounds per day. It isn't much, but we haven't got any overhead." Bledsoe grinned. "I'll get along to headquarters to get things rolling. Zapanta will take care of you lads. I'll try and get more information about your submarine for you."

"Thanks, sir," said Bob.

They watched the powerfully built officer stride toward his headquarters. "He's the best," said the Filipino. "Without him there would be no war here on Mindoro. He was sent here from Luzon to get us organized, and believe me, he *organized* us. Someday that man will be a legend here on Mindoro."

"Like Lieutenant Campos," said Blas.

"And Mang Pedro," said Bob.

Zapanta nodded. "Come on and I'll show you our gasoline-distilling plant. We haven't got much in the way of transportation, but we need gas for what we do have."

A strong smell of liquor spirits hung about the area where the distillery was situated. "Tuba," said Zapanta. "Native booze. Smells bad and kicks harder than an Army mule, but we found a better use for it."

"Looks like the Kentucky hills," said Blas.

"The revenoors never bother us," said Zapanta with a grin. "We distill the tuba through galvanized-iron piping. Tuba is made from the berries of the palm tree. One of the fronds has a little bunch of berries on it. This frond is trained for about two weeks to hang down. In the morning and the evening thin slivers are cut from the berries, and the milk, or sap, bleeds out of them into a small bamboo tub. Pulverized tanbark from the mangrove tree is added as a fermenter and disinfectant. The tuba growers were organized by Colonel Bledsoe, and we pay them fifty centavos for a five-gallon can of the unfermented palm juice. We keep this plant, and several others, hidden in the jungle, running night and day. We can average about five to six gallons a day."

"Must be potent stuff," observed Blas.

"It is. About 90 percent alcohol. We have to open up the gas jets on the carburetors or ream them out to let in more alcohol than gasoline. We can get about six to eight miles per gallon. It's treacherous stuff though. If left uncapped, it absorbs water at a terrific rate, soaking it in right out of the air. Another problem is that the tuba is grown near the coast and distilled there, and the Japs make a practice of finding the distilleries and burning them. It's getting harder and harder to get tuba. If we can't get any more, we'll be out of transportation. We can't bring enough in from submarines, and besides, there are other supplies that we vitally need and gasoline drums take up too much room."

"You need a tanker sub," said Blas wisely.

"*Is* there such a thing as a tanker sub?" asked Zapanta.

"No," said Blas. "But I'll work on it."

Bob was looking curiously at a rather rusted iron wire that was strung from tree to tree. "Those insulators look like pop bottles," he said.

Zapanta nodded. "We don't use that line much anymore. Before we got some radio equipment we had to maintain communications somehow. The Bamboo Telegraph works, but it isn't too fast and isn't always as accurate as we'd like it to be. So Colonel Bledsoe started M.T.&T.—Mindoro Telephone and Telegraph. It took some doing, I'll tell you! We didn't have enough wire, so we took every reel of barbed wire we could find stuck away in some of the old bodegas along the coast and even had to strip it from fence posts to get enough. Then we had to remove the barbs, which we later used as small nails, unwind the wire, and stretch it and spool it. Insulators were out of the question, so we rounded up all the empty pop bottles we could find. They work fine." Zapanta shook his head. "We were hoping for more radios, not only for local use, but also to keep in touch with headquarters. We might have to revert back to the old M.T.&T."

"Any shares left?" asked Blas. "I'd like to get a few blue-chip stocks."

"Now you know why we fight for supplies in this crazy, mixed-up Bamboo War," said the Filipino. "That's why we have to strike the Hapons where they are weak. We can't afford to attack them in fortified positions. We have enough men, but not enough ammunition to expend."

"That was the mistake Lieutenant Campos made," said Blas. "Only his *boroba* thought better of it. He was a brave man."

Zapanta nodded. "He went loco. He forgot how badly we needed those supplies. It is too bad everything was lost. We gained nothing and lost two fine men because of that attack. Perhaps he had been fighting here too long. He went in and out of here several times on your submarines and could have stayed out, to help train agents to work underground here on Mindoro, but he would not stay there. He made one trip too many. One cannot look into the face of death too many times, else it will take you."

"Amen," said Blas.

Zapanta led them to a small, newly constructed hut placed under the trees, well concealed from the air. "These are my quarters," he said. "You are welcome to share them with me."

"There are two beds," said Bob. "Maybe it would be too crowded for you and your bunkie."

Zapanta shook his head, "No," he said quietly. "Fred Campos was my bunkie. See you later, fellows." He walked quickly away.

"That was bright of me," said Bob.

Blas slapped his shoulder. "You didn't know, kid," he said. "Let's take it easy until chow time."

The hut was neat and clean, made much the same as the one they had used while staying with the Mangyans. "Man," said Bob, "this *is* bamboo country. They seem to make nearly everything out of it."

The hut was made of bamboo, vines, and cogongrass. The walls were of sawali, or woven split bamboo, and the roof was of thatched cogongrass. There wasn't a nail in the place, for everything was bound together by vines.

"Listen!" said Blas.

The faint, intermittent sound of an airplane engine came drifting over the hills toward them. It came closer and closer until the sound of it filled the valley in which the barrio was sited.

Someone struck the biggest church bell three times with the metal hammer, and those Filipinos who had been out in the open immediately sought cover. Bob and Blas ran in under the trees. There wasn't a living soul to be seen in or near the barrio.

The engine roared overhead, and the plane banked with the sun flashing from the greenhouse atop it. It was so low that Bob could see the grease and oil that stained the fuselage back of the engine.

"Man," said Blas, "you could strike a match on his pontoons as they go by."

The plane swung away and circled, then came in again, until the roaring of the big engine was deafening. Bob could see several small, fat bombs hanging beneath the fuselage. An uncomfortable feeling came over him. One bomb like that might lay half the bamboo buildings of the barrio flat on the ground.

The plane circled for five more minutes and then flew off down the wide valley toward the sparkling South China Sea. Before the sound of the engine had died away the church bell was tapped once, and the barrio came alive again.

Bob and Blas tried to sleep, but someone was pounding on metal somewhere nearby. Every now and then an argument in shrill, vituperative Filipino would break out, only to die away, and then the metal-pounding would begin again.

Blas sat up and shook his head. "I can't sleep with that going on."

"Let's take a look-see," said Bob.

They left the hut and walked across the street to where a roof of thatched cogongrass stood on four rickety poles. Under it was a battered, oil-stained table and half a dozen Filipinos, including a buxom woman. A young American wearing a battered, shapeless Air Corps cap was watching the Filipinos with an amused look on his face.

"What's going on, Mac?" asked Blas.

"This is the local Aberdeen Proving Ground," said the American. "Mama Rosalia has this as a pet project, and no one can convince her she *can't* make a cannon. I'm Jerry

Hoffman, U.S. Air Corps, ordnance adviser to this crazy, mixed-up *boroba*. They listen to all I tell them and then go right ahead and do as they please. When Mama Rosalia makes up her mind, it's Alibongbong."

"Bob Dunbar, U.S.N.," said Bob. "This is my shipmate Stan Blascovitz. What's Alibongbong, Jerry?"

The young man grinned. "That's Mama's last name. Señora Rosalia Loling Nonita Margherita *Alibongbong!* She's the combined cook, nurse, chaplain, mechanic, inventor, and general all-around lady of all work in this *boroba*. So, when you want anything done chop-chop, you just say it's Alibongbong. Can do! She's a great old gal. The little skinny guy looking like a wet and half-starved chicken is Papa Alibongbong. He's scared to death of her, but I think it is one of the great love stories of all time, like Romeo and Juliet, Hero and Leander, Lord Nelson and Lady Hamilton. You know."

Mama Alibongbong flashed the two onlookers a toothy smile. "Hiya, kiddos," she said. "You know anything about cannons, hey?"

Bob caught a look from Jerry and shook his head.

"*Bahála ná!* Mama Rosalia will makee-do!"

"She's worth a platoon in action," said Jerry. "Talk about an Amazon. But if anyone gets wounded, Mama Rosalia is as tender as a saint. If this hole-in-the-pants, banana-eating army ever had a living spirit and morale, it's Mama Rosalia Alibongbong."

The barrel of the cannon was a three-inch gas pipe with metal rings and bands about the barrel for reinforcement. Metal wedges had been tapped in under the rings and bands to make them tighter. Half a dozen pieces of brass tubing or pipe were being worked into shells for the cannon. A battered wash pan sat in front of serious-faced Papa Alibongbong, from which he selected various items such as chunks of battery lead, babbitt metal, rusty nails, screws and bolts, unidentifiable pieces of jagged metal, and all sorts of odds and ends. He took out a set of false teeth, studied them gravely and dropped them into the shell casing. A metal disk had been welded onto the bottom of each shell casing and through it protruded a piece of smaller pipe.

Jerry spoke out of the side of his mouth. "I've been trying to tell them about the propelling charge, but they won't buy it. That's powder from a Jap mine. That tube inside the shell is crammed with it. Now watch! Mama Rosalia is going to make a primer. Be ready to hit the dirt!"

The big woman took three shotgun shells from a faded box and began to force them into the tube that ran into the center of the shell casing. It was a ticklish job, and if they exploded she might kill herself, or at least lose a hand, but there was no fear on the face of Mrs. Alibongbong— which is more than you could say for her husband and protector, Papa Alibongbong, and the three Americans who watched her uneasily.

Blas looked curiously at the firing pin of the cannon. It was an old marlinspike given tension by thick rubber bands cut from an inner tube.

"The spike has to go through all three shotgun shells to ignite the charge," said Jerry. "Man, I hope I'm nowhere near that crazy thing when it goes off. It'll probably do more damage *behind* it than *ahead* of it!"

Mama Rosalia took the primer and tapped it lightly into place while a young Filipino whittled wooden wedges to hold the dangerous and powerful primer in place. Bob wiped the icy sweat from his forehead. Watching her load one primer was enough, and there were five more shells to be serviced. He walked away from the busy people in the shed. Three Filipinos were working on the gun carriage, which was mounted on thick wooden wheels like an old *carreta*. Bob remembered that there had been some bazookas and mortars unloaded from *Grayfin*. He wondered where they were now. They sure could be used. He began to realize thoroughly how really important those supplies had been.

"Bob!" called out Colonel Bledsoe.

Bob whirled. "Sir?" he said.

The officer slowed down from his rapid walk. "I've just got news over the M.T.&T. that our spies think they have found out where the Hapons took those radios from *Grayfin*."

"Yes, sir," said Bob with a puzzled look on his face.

"Do you think you can find the place where those supplies were cached?"

"I can try, sir. But haven't the Hapons taken them all away?" said Bob.

"We don't know for sure. Our spies say they brought in some gear from the jungle and think it is in the barrio where Campos got himself killed. I might have time to get down there and check to see if they got it all. If they haven't, we might be fortunate enough to get at least one radio out of the deal."

Blas walked toward them. "And if you don't, sir?" he asked.

Bledsoe shrugged. "Then we go in and try to take one away from the Hapons. Trouble is, I haven't got enough men here to do the job. I want them to stay on the ammunition-making deal."

"Mama Alibongbong will go!" shouted the courageous woman. She slapped the breech of the cannon. "This will make up for the lack of soldiers, Colonel!"

Bledsoe looked questioningly at Bob. "Will you two volunteer to go? Lieutenant Morelos must remain here in

86

charge. That leaves only you and Blas who know where the cache is."

"Volunteer?" said Blas. "I never did it in my life, sir, and I'm not about to start now."

Bledsoe's face flushed. "I can't *order* you and Dunbar to go," he said stiffly.

"You don't have to order *me*, sir," said Bob. He looked coldly at Blas.

Blas grinned. "Oh," he said casually, "I *want* to go, but I just didn't want to spoil a perfect record of three enlistments without volunteering once."

Bob smiled. Bledsoe looked at Blas. "I hereby *order* you to go!" he snapped, going along with the joke.

Blas shrugged resignedly. "Well, you can't win 'em all," he said.

"It will take us a long time to get back there, sir," said Bob.

"No," said Bledsoe. "We'll truck out of here as soon as it's dark and drive down to the coast. The Coconut Patrol will take us south along the coast until we reach the river. The barrio where Campos was killed is on that river. We can go up it by banca, stop short of the barrio and take off through the jungle to find the cache."

"Just like that," breathed Blas.

"You've got a better way?" said Bob.

"No."

"Then we go the colonel's way!" said Bob.

They spent the remaining hours of daylight getting their gear ready. Bob and Blas drew jungle boots and fresh cotton uniforms from the meager supplies. Bob got extra magazines and cartridges for his carbine, and Blas drew a tommy gun. The jungle was suddenly dark as though someone had dropped a curtain over it. The thudding, clanking, and banging indicated that Mama Rosalia was having her beloved cannon loaded in the back of one of the battered trucks that ran on the potent tuba gas. Woe betide the man who damaged her cannon. She would rather have seen Papa Alibongbong get scratched than her artillery.

Colonel Bledsoe came through the darkness. "We'll meet some of the boys from another *boroba* when we reach the river," he said. "Likely only a handful but we'll makee-do. *Alibongbong!*"

They swung up into the rear of the truck, and the engine coughed, spluttered, wheezed, and finally kicked over with a rattling roar. The truck, sagging low on one broken spring, sort of waddled out onto the road, and the Filipino driver took off down the hill as though he were getting up enough speed to plane down to the beach.

Blas settled himself on the hard seat beside Mama Rosalia. "You know something?" he said thoughtfully.

"What, kiddo?" said Mama.

"I think this crazy truck is drunk," said the cook.

Mama Rosalia roared. A hamlike hand came down on Blas' thigh with a cracking sound. He paled at the shock of it. Bob nearly fell over the rusted, battered tailgate of the truck laughing at the pained look on the big cook's face. He might just have met his match in Mama Rosalia Alibongbong.

8 . . .

I<small>T WAS</small> still very dark when the truck ground to a lurch-ing halt not far from the mouth of a creek shielded by mangrove trees. Shadowy figures moved here and there in the darkness. There was a rank, strong odor of rotting vegetation, salt, and mud. The dry palm leaves rattled in the shifting wind. Bob could make out a pair of forty-foot outriggered bancas. Both of them were two-masted and lateen rigged. Mama Rosalia's cannon was loaded into one of the bancas.

"We've got several hours before the moon rises," said Jim Bledsoe. "Enough time to beat it down the coast. We'll hole up in a mangrove swamp until the moon dies. We should make the rendezvous by dawn."

The guerrillas stood around listening to him as the banca men eased the grounded heavy log craft into deeper water. There were no more than twenty all told, some of them having been waiting near the bancas for Bledsoe and his men to join them. Not very many to attack a Japa-nese-held barrio, thought Bob.

Bledsoe slung his BAR over his shoulder. He looked up at the dark sky through the waving palm fronds. "You boys know the rules," he said. "If you get captured and think they can make you talk, you realize what will happen to the rest of us and the boys waiting down the coast for us. We've got to get at least one of those radios."

It was very quiet except for the dry rustling of the leaves and the faint sound of the surf washing the beaches at the mouth of the creek. A man coughed. Feet shuffled in the sand. The men did not look at each other in the darkness.

Bledsoe stepped into the water and looked back. "If one is not strong enough to keep quiet when the Hapons question him, it is better that they *cannot* question him. *Los muertos no hablan, amigos.*" He waded out to the first banca and got into it.

Blas slung his tommy gun and looked at Bob. "What does that mean, kid?" he asked.

Bob struggled with his high school Spanish. "The dead do not talk," he said quietly.

"Yeh," said Blas thoughtfully. "Well, come on. Those bancas aren't exactly fleet-type subs but anyway we'll be back on water where we belong."

They waded out to a banca and climbed in just in front of the cannon. Mama Rosalia sat next to it, a thick arm flung over the barrel. Now and then she patted it. The look on her broad, round face boded no good for the Hapons once Mama Rosalia touched off her beloved cannon.

They paddled out to the mouth of the creek and met the sea wash, rising and falling, until they passed into easier water and paddled between rows of bamboo fish traps. Once beyond the traps, they hoisted the triangular sails which rose higher than the slender masts, and the breeze filled the sails. Swiftly the bancas plunged out into the darkness of the open sea with the outriggers rising and falling with the tilt of the bancas. In the stern of each banca sat the helmsman, steering by means of a tiller, although how they knew where they were going was beyond Bob. But they knew these waters, as their fathers and

90

grandfathers had known them before their time, and as their sons and grandsons would know them, for such was their tradition, and a proud one it was.

When water slopped over the side, the guerrillas bailed with *bagools,* which were coconut shells cut in half, with wooden handles attached. When the breeze freshened, some of the men had to run out on the dangerously tilting outriggers to force them down again, and the Coconut Patrol bancas skimmed through the darkness like things alive.

It felt good to be at sea again after the swamps and the festering jungles, thought Bob. The sea breeze dried the sweat on his face and hair and every so often spray would strike him. He shielded his carbine from it and looked at Blas. Blas was in his element, although he had probably spent more time underwater during his enlistments than he had on top of it. Still, he *was* a sailor, and a sailor is only really home at sea.

Bob looked at the other banca and saw the solid figure of Colonel Bledsoe. The officer's words came back to him on the soft wind: *"Los muertos no hablan, amigos."* Suddenly he felt cold.

The shoreline was a dark blur to port as the bancas plunged on through the sea. There wasn't a light to be seen, although there were shacks and barrios all along that coast. Perhaps the Filipinos had left them, *buqwee-ing* ahead of the Hapons. The civilians were suffering between the Hapons and the guerrillas, as all civilians did in such a type of warfare. It was deadly, cruel, and merciless, and The Aid, promised by the *americanos,* was dribbling into the islands in very small quantities. No one knew for sure what was happening in the outside world. The Japanese radio broadcasts in Spanish and in the various dialects of the many islands indicated that everywhere the forces of Nippon were victorious. The United States fleet had never recovered from the Hawaiian debacle at Pearl Harbor. The United States Marines had been cut off on Guadalcanal and were surrendering daily. Japanese forces in the Aleutians were almost ready to step ashore on the Alaskan mainland, and from there it was only a hop, skip, and jump down to the West Coast. Already Japanese submarines had swept much of the merchant fleet of the United States away from the West Coast, and brave submarine commanders and crews of Dai Nippon had boldly surfaced and shelled Los Angeles and San Francisco. And so on and so on.

Bob thought of the battered and invincible *Grayfin*. The biggest mistake the enemy had made in their secret war plans was in not knocking out the fleet-type submarines at Pearl and in not destroying the huge supply of fuel there. It was the submarines that had carried the war to the Japanese. There had been fifty-one of them in the Pacific when the war had started, and the Japanese had considered them inconsequential. They couldn't have made a bigger mistake. Few of the submarines had been at Pearl on December 7, 1941—five to be exact, and most of them undergoing repairs. None of them had been damaged. The Japanese had had myopia where the submarines were concerned. Still thinking in terms of capital ships, they had concentrated on the battle wagons, with devastating effect. But the U.S.S. *Pollack* was already cruising off Honshu on New Year's Eve of 1941. On January 7, 1942, she had sunk a Japanese ship.

"Look!" said Mama Rosalia.

Bob looked up in time to see a faint winking of light across the dark waters. There wasn't any doubt in his mind that it was a signal lamp. Maybe it was *Grayfin!*

"No, kid," said Blas over his shoulder. "*Grayfin* wouldn't be signaling. That's more likely a Nip patrol boat."

The cook had read Bob's mind. He should have known better. *Grayfin* was well on her way to Port Darwin by now. The light winked on and off again. Then it was dark.

"Run in closer to shore!" called out Colonel Bledsoe.

Obediently the bancas turned and skimmed in toward the dark shoreline. The water became rougher in the shallows, the bancas pitched and heaved wildly, and time and time again the crewmen had to run out on the outriggers to keep them from rising too high out of the water. The *bagools* dipped steadily, flinging the water over the side.

Bob kept on bailing even while looking back toward that mysterious winking light. Suddenly it was gone completely in the velvety darkness. Bob remembered uncomfortably something Zapanta Morelos had said. "They run patrol boats through the passages. Subchasers armed with machine guns and 75mm. guns. I personally haven't seen any of their submarines out there but some of the others have, and of course there is always their air patrol."

"There is the light again," said Stan. He placed his tommy gun in his lap. It wouldn't be of much value against a subchaser. The winking light was much closer and another one appeared even nearer to the racing bancas. Stan whistled softly.

Swiftly the crews hauled down the lateen sails. Paddles dipped overside. The bancas were low in the water and too dark to see; but if the Japanese had radar, which wasn't likely, they might pick up a pair of tiny pips on their screens. A shaft of brilliant light stabbed out of the darkness and lanced just behind the wallowing bancas. The searchlight swung left instead of right. The patrol boat was hardly two hundred yards away.

Bob swallowed hard. His throat went dry, and his blood seemed to turn into icy mush and his stomach to roll uneasily over. He had visions of the bancas being smashed by shellfire and the struggling crews picked off by machine guns.

The bancas seemed stuck in black molasses although the paddles rose and fell like pistons. The surf was crashing on the beach and withdrawing with a dragging roar, and it was very close.

"They might not spot us," said Blas.

The cook had hardly closed his mouth when the searchlight swung right and stabbed its icy light right on the two bancas. A Chicago piano—a Japanese pompom—broke into gobbling life *poomp-poomp-poomp-poomp-poomp* and orange-blue tracers swept arclike out toward the bancas. A Filipino screamed once, went over the side, and did not come up. Slugs whipped through the aftermast of Bledsoe's banca and felled it.

"If I could only shoot!" screamed Mama Rosalia in frustration.

Their strained faces were a ghastly bluish white in the searchlight glare, as though they were already dead. There was no hope for them; no hope at all. Farther offshore a crumping sound came, followed by an angry reddish-orange burst of flame and a rushing sound overhead. Between the bancas and the shore a shimmering white tree shot mysteriously up out of the water.

Jim Bledsoe stood up calmly in the pitching banca, facing right into the tracers. He raised his heavy BAR and sighted it. With a blurting roar he emptied the twenty-round magazine. The searchlight dimmed and turned orange, then red, and then died out altogether. At the same time the patrol boat struck heavily and listed to one side.

"She's aground!" said Bledsoe. "Get up those sails! They won't bother about us now! They won't want her sitting there in the morning right under the noses of the Filipinos."

94

The sails crept up and the breeze filled them. Bob's banca shot ahead, for the other banca had lost her aftermast, but still she put on a good turn of speed. Behind them in the night the signal lamps winked back and forth between the two patrol boats. Bob grinned. They seemed angrier than they had been before.

The guerrillas spent the next hour whittling plugs and hammering them into the bullet holes in the bancas while some bailed steadily. When Bob raised his head at last, they were out of sight of the signal lamps. There was a faint, almost imperceptible tinge of light in the eastern sky. Moonrise.

By the time the moon shed enough light to reach the western shore of Mindoro, the bancas were being pushed and dragged through the shallows into the cover of the swamp growths. They rested on the muddy bottom in several inches of water. In a little while the moonlight turned the upper leaves of the palm trees farther along the shore into a million glittering blades, and the sand of the beaches was as white as snow, darkly etched with tree shadows.

"Two dead," said Jim Bledsoe. He lighted a cigar and flipped the match into the water where it died with a hiss. "Not bad at that. Only by the grace of God did the rest of us get away."

"That and some of the best shooting I've ever seen," said Blas.

Bledsoe shook his head. "It was the grounding that saved us." He looked thoughtfully at the makeshift cannon. "If we didn't have to get down south," he said wistfully, "we sure could raise a little trouble with that crazy cannon."

Mama Rosalia slapped at a mosquito. "Maybe we got time, yes? We could sneak back along the shore and reach there after moonset. How could we miss, my colonel?"

Bledsoe shook his head. "Stop eating of the fire, Mama Rosalia. What we have to do down south is far more important than dusting up a Jap patrol boat. Man, it *does* make you itch just thinking of it."

It was very quiet for a long time after that. Most of the Filipinos slept. The wind rustled dryly through the leaves. The insect song was continuous and at times almost overwhelming, rising and falling. The wet *click-click* of the crabs came from the mud beyond the grounded bancas. Once a plane droned high overhead, probably heading for Manila. The mosquitoes sent out a call for reinforcements and happily set to work on the helpless people in the bancas, and the sound of slapping increased as the night wore on.

A hard hand gripped Bob's shoulder. "Rise and shine, kid. Show a leg!" It was Blas. Bob opened his eyes. The moon was gone and darkness had filled the world of Mindoro once again. They slid over the side into the warm river, knee-deep in stinking swamp muck and a few inches of muddy water, and manhandled the heavy bancas toward the deeper water, with the sweat breaking out on their straining bodies, stinging the myriad insect bites that tortured them. The bancas began to bob sluggishly up and down. They pulled themselves wearily into the boats. The sails rattled up and the paddles dipped. They swept through the creaming surf to the smoother water, and then the sails filled. No sooner had they steadied on their southward course when Bob dropped exhausted into the bilge of the banca with the muddy, ill-smelling bilge water slopping back and forth beneath him. The banca leaned far over as she sped along with the water hissing softly past her battered and splintered sides. The last thing Bob remembered was the steady sound of the *bagools* striking the bottom of the banca as she was bailed.

9 . . .

THEY WERE waist-deep in water working the heavy bancas back into the tidal swamp that covered both sides of the mouth of the dark river up which was the Japanese-held barrio. It was the time of the dense blackness before the coming of the false dawn. It was very quiet except for the washing of the water against the sides of the bancas and the splashing of the men, while the wind shifted and died away before the coming of the stronger dawn wind.

Bob wiped mud from his face. At least the mosquitoes had quit in the coolness before the dawn. He shivered, although the water was not cold. The thought of malaria drifted through his tired mind. Atabrine and quinine were desperately short in the guerrilla supplies. The *anas*, or malaria mosquitoes, and the germs of dysentery were as deadly to the Bamboo Army as were the Japanese. It was a rough way to fight a war. No medical supplies. No doctors. No hospitals. Nothing except a few dedicated Filipino nurses who took care of the sick and wounded as best they could and sometimes fought beside their men.

Bledsoe whistled sharply three times. The men stopped wading and held the bancas against the sluggish current. Something splashed not far from them. Bob swallowed hard. There was nothing to see except the dark, hooded shapes of the tall trees on each side of the waterway. He looked across at Blas. He could just make out the broad face of the cook, swollen from insect bites. "Maybe only a croc," said Blas cheerfully.

"Quiet!" snapped Mama Rosalia.

Bob rested his head against the side of the boat. He had forgotten about the crocodiles. He remembered all too well seeing the humped eyes and rounded nose tips on the murky green water the first day he had been in the jungle of Mindoro. He remembered the powerful flailing body of the big croc that had been thrown up from the river depths when the Japanese plane had dropped a bomb. Worst of all, he remembered the attack made by a huge croc on one of the helpless carabaos while supplies were being ferried across the river.

Something bumped Bob's side and he sickened within himself as green fear raced through his mind. He almost screamed aloud as his left hand touched a rough, slimy surface and only at the last possible split second he realized it was a log. His heart slammed back and forth until it seemed as though it would burst through the rib cage. Bad as his earlier wartime experiences in the Aleutians had been, he would take the cold and the wet and the roaring storms of the Aleutian Chain in preference to this theater of fighting. His appreciation for the tough, fatalistic Bamboo Warriors of the Mindoro *borobas* was growing by the minute.

The sharp, staccato notes of a bamboo flute echoed through the swamp. Bledsoe waved on his little force. Slowly, almost imperceptibly, the water shallowed until the guerrillas were slogging through stinking, knee-deep mud that sucked at their straining legs like the cups on the tentacles of an octopus. The jungle was alive, thought

Bob. No one could beat the jungle. The mud and the constant wet. The crocodiles, mosquitoes, leeches, and snakes. The malaria, jungle fever, dysentery, and poisoned insect bites. The trails that were hardly visible and that seemed to close up behind a man as he advanced with slashing bolo. The ooze and grip of the foul-smelling mud, and the wet slap of saw-edged leaves. The fighting for breath in the exhausting, fetid air.

"Who wouldn't sell a farm and go to sea?" said Blas. He wiped the mud from his face. "Stick it out, kid! *Bahála ná!*"

Old Blas knew the way Bob was thinking. Bob smiled. He could have done a lot worse in having Blas for a shipmate on this amphibious cruise through the jungles of Mindoro. The thought of Gary came into his mind.

They worked the bancas into the undergrowths just as the first faint light of dawn tinged the eastern sky. By the time the great, silent explosion of the sun filled the sky, the bancas were camouflaged so well that a boat passing on the river not fifty yards away could not detect them.

There was no rest for Jim Bledsoe. By the time the sun was full up he had been long gone into the green jungle to make contact with the other guerrilla force.

"I hope they've got more men than we have," said Blas.

"We've got Mama Rosalia and her cannon," said Bob as he squeezed a swollen insect bite.

"Yeh," said Blas dryly. "That crazy cannon will likely get more of us than it will of them."

The slow hours dragged by like a croc with a broken back. All morning long the insect song arose, and the monkeys and birds kept up their incessant chattering, whistling, crying, and cooing, echoing from one end of the swamp to the other. The heat was like a thick, muggy blanket that hung about the bancas until it seemed as though the men could not breathe its heaviness.

In the middle of the afternoon a slow pounding sound came to them. It was that of an engine chugging closer and closer. There was a vista that opened on a sinuous curve of the greenish waters of the river. A clumsy-looking wooden boat appeared, moving very slowly, parting the water and leaving a sluggish wake behind the blunt stern. Bob had seen such a craft before in the Solomons. He remembered the intelligence reports and photographs of such craft. "Type-A Daihatsu," he said. "An Ogata Hatsudokitei. Large landing barge."

Some of the Filipinos looked at him with respect. Mama Rosalia patted her cannon. A young guerrilla sergeant shook his head despite the look of scorn on the Amazon's broad face.

There were troops in the barge, armed with bayoneted rifles. Their baggy, gray-green uniforms were soaked with great dark patches of sweat. The sun glinted from the eyeglasses many of them wore. A broad-shouldered Japanese squatted beside a heavy machine gun. An officer stood in the stern with field glasses at his eyes; the faded white havelock that he wore hanging from the back of his ill-fitting cap flapped in the hot wind.

"Don't move!" snapped the guerrilla sergeant. He was young Celdron Dongalio, hardly more than nineteen, but he had not earned his stripes because of his two years at the University of Manila. He had earned them the hard way in the jungles and in the fighting for barrios and beaches that the Bamboo Warriors excelled in. Three times he had earned the Purple Heart, although none were issued in the Philippines.

The barge engine was shoved into neutral, and the Daihatsu drifted on the slowly moving current toward the bank beyond which were hidden the two bancas. She grounded gently and half a dozen Hapons leaped over

100

the side into the waist-deep water, holding their slim, bayoneted rifles high over their heads. They waded ashore and at a word from the officer on the deck of the barge, they began to work their way through the undergrowths, poking their vicious razor-edged bayonets here and there. If they spotted the bancas, that heavy Nambu machine gun on the foredeck of the barge would lash the bancas with a hail of bullets. There would be little chance for the guerrillas. Only the deadly jungle behind them might give them a chance of escape.

Water splashed not fifty feet from the bancas, and a heavy-shouldered Hapon stood on a slime-covered log, his tabied feet gripping the slippery surface. He held his rifle at arm's length, with the muzzle and bayonet pointing at one Robert Dunbar, Signalman Second Class, United States Navy, and one badly frightened Seaman First Class. The small caliber of the rifle seemed several times larger than it really was; it looked as big as the muzzle of Bob's grandfather's old .50 caliber Sharps hunting rifle that hung over the fireplace in the Dunbar home in Anchorage.

No one moved. The mosquitoes took advantage and moved in more thickly. An insect worked its way up Bob's jaw and poked inquisitively at the lobe of his right ear, debating whether or not to crawl in and investigate. A leech dropped from a leaf and settled itself comfortably on Bob's left forearm. He didn't feel anything, but he knew the slimy, repulsive thing was already cutting into his blood supply. He looked miserably at Blas. Some unidentified flying insect had settled just below Blas's flattened nose and was inserting his needled proboscis into the sweating flesh.

At the last possible second, when Bob could have screamed with the sheer tension of the moment and possibly have opened fire on the Japanese, the soldier turned

101

and splashed his way through the mud to join his mates. They clambered aboard the barge. The engine was put in gear and the barge slowly slogged its way up the river and out of sight. Bob caught the insect at his ear just as it prepared to enter the inviting canal before it.

The day waned and began to die. Colonel Bledsoe came back with ten guerrillas from another *boroba*. "The rest of them are gathering upriver," he said, "on the far side of the barrio. Not as many as I expected, but enough of them to attack if we get a few breaks. They have only two BAR's and a light machine gun, perhaps half a dozen grenades. We'll move upriver as soon as it gets dark and then hole up for part of the night. I want to hit the barrio just before moonrise. With luck, we can cinch the attack by the time the moon is fully up. We'll need the light. We can't take too long at the job because the Bamboo Telegraph says the Hapons are bringing in Imperial Marines to the barrio. They plan to make a strong point out of it. The Lord knows it's strong enough already. If we don't hit them as soon as we can, we'll never be able to take it."

With the coming of the darkness they dragged the bancas through the mud and water to the river and then paddled them upstream, stopping now and then to listen for the sound of a barge engine, but it never came. In two hours they were in position not far from where Bob and Blas had seen Frederico Campos and Mang Pedro die in vain. All weapons were checked. A few grenades were issued. They waited for the attack signal. Bob and Blas were designated as part of the "support," which consisted of three guerrillas and themselves. In addition, if necessary, they were to help Mama Rosalia's artillery group. An hour before the attack they manhandled the wooden-wheeled cannon into position across a weed-grown field. Faintly through the darkness they could see the concrete blockhouse that was the main citadel of the Japanese defense. The walls were at least a foot thick and were pierced with narrow slits for rifle and machine-gun fire. The roof was covered with rusted iron sheeting as a fire precaution. The door was on the far side. Here and there through the sprawling barrio were other buildings that had been improvised into strong points—the old, thick-walled church and the new schoolhouse. The Bamboo Telegraph had said there were between one hundred to one hundred and fifty troops in the barrio, mostly Koreans and Formosans, the refuse of the Japanese Army, to which were added a number of Filipino BC men—Bureau of Constabulary police—carrying their rusted Enfield rifles, and wearing the uniform of grayish-purple short pants and short-sleeved shirts. The guerrillas did not fear these scum. It was rumored that the Kempetai, the Japanese Gestapo, also had a detachment in the barrio. These were the unbelievably sadistic "thought" police of the Japanese. They were never, under any circumstances, taken prisoner.

Mama Rosalia lovingly inserted one of her brass shells into the muzzle of the cannon and rammed it home with a bamboo rod. She drew back the sharpened marlinspike against the powerful tension of the inner-tube rubber bands and wedged it into position. If it slipped, the whole game would be up. Papa Alibongbong looked admiringly at his formidable spouse. "She is The One," he said in his thin, wavering voice.

"Papa," she said over her shoulder, "stay behind me, loved one. It would kill Mama Rosalia to lose you, my chicken."

"He's likely safer up in *front* of her," said Blas.

The darkness seemed to ease a little. Bob could see the tangles and coils of rusted barbed wire between the blockhouse and the rutted road. It was fully dark and very quiet. A guerrilla, a native of the barrio, had already slipped into the compound from the riverbank, taking his life into his hands. Mama Rosalia uncoiled the thirty-foot lanyard of abacá fiber and lay down behind a log. Papa Alibongbong supervised placing thick branches against the wheels and carriage of the gun to brace it against the shock of recoil, for there was no recoil mechanism.

A turkey gobbled faintly and then stopped. Another sounded off and stopped as quickly as the first had. The lone guerrilla in the village was taking care of the tasty birds, for the Hapons used them as watchdogs, staking them out in clearings. A soft whistle drifted toward the tense guerrillas outside the barrio. Bledsoe nodded. All the turkeys had been silenced. He looked at Bob and grinned. "If we win, we'll have Thanksgiving dinner tomorrow," he said.

Bob grinned back weakly in return. He gripped his carbine and suddenly realized that he could make out objects much more distinctly than before. Fear winged silently across the tops of the trees, to slant down in a motionless glide and settle comfortably on the back of Bob Dunbar. Bob closed his eyes. He had been under fire many times, but no matter how many times he had experienced it, it was always the same; he could not resist fear.

Jim Bledsoe looked at the faintly luminous dial of his watch. "Five minutes," he said quietly. "Mama Rosalia?"

"Yes, my colonel!"

"You are ready with the barrage?"

"Yes, my colonel!"

"You have sighted well?"

"Yes, my colonel!"

"Papa Alibongbong?"

"Yes, my colonel!"

"You are ready as well?"

"That is so, my colonel!"

Blas wet his lips and hefted his tommy gun. He patted the two Japanese grenades he had been issued. "Man," he said softly, "I wish we had a couple of big Marine mortars and some of the leathernecks to handle them. We could clean out that pigpen in five minutes."

"Three minutes," said the colonel.

"I am afraid!" suddenly said young Abundio Campos. He was a cousin to Frederico Campos. He was only sixteen years old.

Sergeant Celdron Dongalio gripped the boy's thin shoulder. "See the wire, soldier? That is where your cousin died fighting the Hapons! Perhaps the very Hapons who killed him are in that blockhouse!"

Abundio nodded miserably. He gripped his heavy Enfield rifle in his small hands. He had only a full clip and after that he would have to arm himself with a Japanese weapon.

"Two minutes!" said the colonel.

It was growing lighter. A rooster suddenly crowed somewhere in among the shacks of the barrio.

Bob looked back over his shoulder. The trees were a good fifty yards behind them. Only one thin tree stood near the log where Mama Alibongbong was ready with her lanyard in hand. If the attack broke on the wire, not a man would reach those trees alive. The Japanese probably had that open field taped to the inch. He looked toward the barrio. Dimly seen at the edge of the river, beyond the blockhouse, was the big Daihatsu barge. A man stood on the foredeck beside the heavy Nambu machine gun.

"One minute!" said the colonel inexorably.

Bob got up on one knee and raised his carbine. It seemed

pitifully small and weak compared to the heavy weapons of the Japanese.

Bledsoe unslung his BAR. Abundio Campos stepped up close behind the tall officer, carrying a canvas harness with four full magazines for the BAR. Sergeant Dongalio picked up the heavy, long-handled wire cutters with which he was equipped. He winked at Bob. He wasn't much older than Bob.

"Time!" barked the colonel. "*Alibongbong!*"

Mama Rosalia jerked the abacá-fiber lanyard.

10 . . .

THERE WAS a smashing, flame-tipped discharge from the cannon. "Now!" yelled the colonel. "*Sigi legi, ho!*" "Alibongbong!" roared the guerrillas. They swept down toward the barrio through the swirling smoke from the cannon discharge. Bob glanced back as he ran after the others. The cannon had flip-flopped backward and had bounced from the resilient earth and was flying back through the air toward the yelling crew. The barrel had peeled back like a banana. The crew scattered as the Nambu on the deck of the barge opened chattering fire across the field toward the ruined gun, ignoring the obvious, the swift-running attack led by Colonel Bledsoe.

A hole smoked in the wall of the blockhouse. But for some reason or other the blockhouse was silent, with smoke seeping from the gun slits. Bledsoe opened fire on a trio of running Japanese and the concentrated smashing power of the BAR swept them off their feet, with their bandy legs still churning air. He jerked free the empty magazine and Abundio Campos, his fear forgotten, rammed in a full magazine.

Sergeant Dongalio hurled himself at the wire, and heedless of the rusted barbs, began to cut his way through the wire with professional skill. Three more Japanese ran into the open, hauling a light machine gun. Blas hurled a grenade and emptied a full drum of .45 caliber stuff into them from his tommy gun.

The church bell began to ring. A squad of Japanese racing toward the wire turned almost as one man and ran back toward the church, firing wildly in all directions. Bob looked back over his shoulder and couldn't help grinning. The cannon lay ignominiously on its back, smoking a little from the peeled barrel. The gallant gun crew, led by Papa Alibongbong, were all trying to get behind the one thin tree. But a stout figure was running clumsily, though swiftly, through the sharp-edged cogongrass, which was ripping her faded dress to pieces. It was Mama Rosalia. She held a grenade in each strong hand. The Nambu on the barge swung to fire at the guerrillas cutting through the wire. Before the gun flashed into life a grenade flew through the air and burst inside the barge. The gunner staggered and swung the gun to cover Mama Rosalia just in time to have a grenade strike his face and explode. He went over backward into the dark green waters.

The wire snapped loose and curled back on itself, and Jim Bledsoe plunged through it as though meeting the curl of a wave. He shook out a full magazine of .30/06, and Abundio Campos refueled the smoking BAR. "The schoolhouse!" yelled Bledsoe. "That's where the radios are! Go get 'em. Chop-chop!"

It was much lighter now. Guns chattered and grenades coughed from the other end of the village where the other *boroba* was striking.

Bob ran toward the schoolhouse. Flames licked up from a shack on stilts. Glass shattered in another building. A grenade flashed inside another shack, and smoke billowed from the windows. Bob felt better now. The heat and excitement of action had burned the fear out of him or had at least pushed it aside. Long sparks sailed over his head above the swirling smoke as the thatched roof of the burning shack began to go, with flames dancing crazily out of the holes while others licked hungrily up the bone-dry split-bamboo sides. He leaped over the sprawled body of a BC man. He fired twice at a screaming soldier but did not see whether he fell because of the swirling smoke. A man could die in a hurry that dawn.

Somewhere a Japanese NII mortar coughed, and the projectile burst right in the midst of a knot of screaming BC men, scattering them like tenpins. Bolos flashed as the guerrillas who had run out of ammunition went into action with the weapon they loved the best—as a Scots Highlander loves his broad-bladed claymore and deadly dirk. Not for nothing had the Bamboo Warriors called their units Bolo Battalions.

Squads of Japanese broke from the cover of the trees along the lightening river, charging sturdily up the muddy slope, long bayonets thirsting for Filipino blood. "Banzai! Banzai! Banzai!" they yelled hoarsely. A grenade burst among them, A Japanese light Nambu chattered into life manned by Sergeant Dongalio. Bob jumped between two shacks. He was cut off. He crouched and ran toward the river to get behind them. He saw a line of stilted shacks with excited chickens beneath them. As he turned to round a shack he looked full into the faces of two tough Japanese soldiers. They set themselves and charged. He swung his rusty carbine, and it jammed on the first shot. There was no time to run. No place to go. Green fear flew in again, searching for Bob Dunbar.

An automatic weapon stuttered from the far side of the shack, pouring a hail of bullets right under the shacks, scattering chickens to all sides in a shower of detached feathers. One Japanese fell, coughing harshly. The second was wounded. He turned and raised his Arisaka rifle. Bob stepped in close and smashed the butt of his carbine at the nape of the man's neck, and he went down flat on his face.

An odd-looking figure charged through the excited chickens with a smoking tommy gun in his hands. "You all right, Little Brown Brother?" a familiar voice said.

Bob stared. The man wore a peaked woven-straw Filipino hat, from the brim of which depended little red-dyed woolen or cotton balls on strings. A *barong tagalog*, or filmy embroidered shirt, hung outside the mud-caked trousers. Shoes soled with rubber from tires were on his feet. Half a dozen extra magazines for the submachine gun clattered together from where they hung by cords about his neck and over his shoulders. A huge bolo was thrust through a mold-green GI web belt, and some Japanese grenades hung by cords from the belt.

"Old *Bahála ná!*" yelled Bob. "Gary! Where did *you* come from?"

Gary stared at Bob. "I don't believe it," he said slowly. "They said you had been killed on the beach." Gary passed a dirty claw over his eyes. "This smoke is rough on the eyes," he added quickly.

Bob gripped his shipmate. The magazines clattered. "For a minute I thought you were Joe Filipino himself."

Gary busied himself replacing his empty magazine. "No time for scuttlebutt," he said. "Got to get one of those radios."

Bob picked up the light Arisaka of one of the fallen Japs and helped himself to ammunition. He took off the bayonet and threw it away. The second Japanese had a Nambu pistol in a clamshell holster. It was fully loaded, with two extra clips in the holster.

They ran through the swirling smoke to the schoolhouse. A grenade sailed through a window and coughed inside. A Filipino thrust a BAR inside and emptied a full twenty-

110

round magazine into the smoking interior. A darkly tanned American officer kicked open the door and charged in, spraying the interior with tommy-gun fire. Then it was quiet inside. "All right, you bolos!" yelled the officer. "Come and get this radio out of here!"

"That looked like Lieutenant Phil Kelly," said Bob.

"You're very observant," Gary said.

Jim Bledsoe strode through the smoke with Abundio Campos trotting behind him. "*Sigi legi, ho!*" he snapped. "Get a move on! We've just got time to get out of here with that radio! Some of the boys have cleaned the Japs out of that landing barge. We'll run it downriver and sink it to block the channel. The rest of you get that radio gear out of there! Round up some carabaos! Chop-chop! This smoke will be seen for miles when it is full daylight, and the Hapons will be upon us like mad hornets! *Sigi legi, ho!*"

There was no need for him to spur his men on. Sporadic gunfire broke out, now and then punctuated by the crumping of grenades. The guerrillas were cleaning out the Japanese that had not broken for the jungle. A boatload of Japanese trying to cross the river had been sunk by gunfire with no survivors. In twenty minutes, just long enough to get the radio loaded onto a carabao cart and to gather up whatever Japanese weapons and grenades they could find, the guerrillas were ready to move.

"Watch it, lady!" called out Gary as Mama Rosalia came through the smoke. "Old lady like you oughta get under cover. You could get hurt out here. Us guerrillas will protect you. Never fear."

"*Gracias,* friend," she said. "I was afraid, but now that I know you are here to protect an old lady, I have not the fear anymore."

Gary smiled and waved an expansive hand. "Think nothing of it, ma'am," he said. "Always ready to oblige in helping the weak and the old."

111

Blas limped through the smoke carrying a light Nambu machine gun. "Listen to him," he said to Bob. He rolled his eyes upward. "I was hoping he got away on *Grayfin*. No such luck."

Gary rubbed his dirty face. "Well, I *did* say I'd take care of the old and weak, Blas. You want me to help you carry that chopper?"

Blas grinned. He put a bearlike arm around Gary. "I knew something was missing. Now that you're here, shipmate, you must meet Eugene."

"Eugene?" said Gary.

Blas nodded. "My cousin Eugene. Reminds me a lot of you, kid."

"I didn't know you had relatives on Mindoro," said Gary.

"Hundreds of them," said Blas. He winked at Bob.

Sergeant Dongalio came through the smoke. "All cleaned out, sir," he said to Colonel Bledsoe. "About fifty of them broke for the jungle. We let them go. They won't be back. We'll save ammo that way, sir. The jungle should take care of them all within a few days."

Bob shivered a little. He looked at the encroaching green wall of the jungle beyond the weedy field. In that green, wet, mildewed tangle some of the Japanese would die slowly of disease while others might die swiftly and horribly. The first step was to get lost, and probably they were still running deep into what they thought was safety from the Bamboo Warriors. It might have been better for them to return and die swiftly and cleanly by gunfire. Everything looked alike in the jungle. One trail was the same as another. A man could die a hundred yards from a well-traveled road or river and never know it. Fear would drive them on; exhaustion would slow them down; the jungle would move in for the kill.

There were only a few villagers in the barrio. They snatched up what few possessions they wanted to take

112

away and shoved off in their small barotos to travel to the next barrio upriver which was not as yet occupied by the Hapons. Behind them the flames licked steadily at their homes. Great fat sparks sailed up through the thickening pall of smoke. A wall crashed. A roof fell in with a gush of smoke and a shower of swirling sparks.

In a little while the barge went downriver to be sunk as a block ship in the channel. It would take the Japanese days to remove it, and if they landed beyond it and walked toward the barrio, it would take them half a day to get there, never knowing whether or not the guerrillas were waiting to ambush them.

The sun was well up when the guerrillas pulled out, heading up the road toward the distant green-clad hills. Behind them something exploded in the village, scattering burning wood and sparks over the roofs of the shacks that were not yet alight. In five minutes the whole barrio was ablaze and roaring.

Mama Rosalia trudged alongside a carabao which was hauling a rickety cart upon which jolted her beloved cannon with its fringed muzzle. Papa Alibongbong trudged behind her with a downcast look on his face. Some day he would prove to Mama that he too was a hero. It was just that his luck was bad.

"Some cannon," said Gary with a grin.

Blas shook his head. "Don't underestimate that crazy thing," he said. "I looked into that blockhouse. The floor was covered with dead and dying Japs. It punched a hole about six inches across going in and hit the far wall before it exploded. It was like a mincer in there, fellows. I never saw anything like it."

There was a proud look on the face of Mama Rosalia Loling Nonita Margherita Alibongbong, the heroine of the day. One shot from her cannon had done more damage than all the guerrillas' fire put together.

11 . . .

THE RADIO SHACK was in a semiclearing up on the slopes of the higher land that overlooked the sea which sparkled brightly so far, far below. It was a simple structure, put up in jig time by the little Mangyans, with a bamboo pole in each corner and two in the center, with thick leaves for a roof, and secured with rattan vines. The floor was also of bamboo, fresh smelling and green. The bright new radio sat on a solidly constructed bamboo bench with two puzzled-looking characters staring at it. Gary rubbed his lean face. "Maybe it's the aerial?" he said.

"Tell Abundio to shift it to a taller tree," said Bob.

Gary stuck his head out of the side of the house. "Hey, Abundio!" he yelled. "Try that next tree! It's at least fifteen feet higher!"

Abundio shrugged. He went up the tree as if he were walking up it. He loosened the aerial and dropped it. He came swiftly down the tree and started up the next one with the aerial tied to his belt. At the top of the tree he began to jerk around, almost falling from the tree.

"What's wrong?" yelled Gary.

"Ants!" cried the young Filipino. "Ants with *teeth!*"

"Stick with it, kid," said Gary. "Got to take a *little* hardship here in this easy war in a tropical paradise. Look at me! Am *I* complaining? Stick to it, *amigo!*"

Bob looked at him in disgust. "You've had that kid climbing every tree within fifty yards of here."

"Well, we got to get this thing working, don't we?"

Bob nodded. They had been on the jungle trails for ten days getting the precious radio to the new base set up by Lieutenant Zapanta Morelos. All their troubles were over now, or so they thought. The radio seemed perfect, the very essence of American production. Well-made, efficiently cased, solid, and destruction resistant. In short, everything a field radio should be. Only one thing was really wrong with it—it didn't work.

Bob shifted in his seat and stared at the implacable face of the radio. "How did I ever get mixed up in this anyway?" he said.

"Because you're a signalman," said Gary. He examined his fingernails with deep interest. "Hey, Abundio! Snap it up with that aerial!"

"It's up!" yelled Abundio through the window.

Gary jumped a foot up from his seat. "Take it easy," he growled.

"Mama Rosalia wants a gunner to help her," said Abundio. "I said I would look around for one." He eyed Gary speculatively.

Gary paled. "I was a cook," he said.

"Cook striker," said Blas from the doorway.

Gary seemed to shrink a little. "Hey, Blas! You wouldn't tell her, would you?" he pleaded.

Blas grinned wolfishly. "Not yet," he said. "She thinks you're a *radioman*. Fancy that!"

"Who is?" said Bob in disgust.

"You worked on radios in the Solomons, didn't you?" said Blas. He fed Eugene a scrap of food. Eugene chattered happily.

Bob nodded. "Yeh. An Australian 3B. But it wasn't anything like this one. I'm beat, Blas."

"Let's kick over the generator and try again," said Gary. "Maybe shifting the aerial will make the difference."

Bob looked at him. "You and that crazy aerial," he said. "I've been trying to tell you it's something else."

Blas squatted in the doorway. "Of all the breaks," he said. "They brought in a couple more radios a few days ago . . . ATR's. It was *Nautilus* brought them in. Big deal! They loaded each of them in a different banca to make sure *one* of them got ashore. The surf was running high after the *Chibasco* that hit. Out of about fifty bancas two got sunk. Guess what two?"

Bob stood up and walked outside. He looked gloomily at the generator and engine. It was an old Fairbanks-Morse set up for running the only hair-curling machine in northern Mindoro. The hair-curling machine had run on 110 volts alternating current and the broadcast set in the hut required 220 volts. It had taken Gary, Blas, Abundio, and Bob five days winding and rewinding the transformer to step up the voltage. But nothing worked. He was about ready to give up.

"*Bahála ná!*" yelled Sergeant Dongalio. "Perceive!"

A file of guerrillas staggered along with poles on their shoulders cutting deeply into the flesh. Depending from one set of poles were several heavy boxes, and from the other set a transformer and some other gear hung heavily.

"How's this for a stroke of luck?" said the Filipino. "You got the only hair-curling machine on northern Mindoro which isn't any good and we come up with the only stepped-down transformer on northern Mindoro. Used for the lone motion-picture projector within a hundred miles. Converts from 110 volts to 220!"

Bob raised his eyes to the bright sky. "I don't believe it!" he cried. "This is too much!"

Gary came out of the shack and went to work on the

116

cranky engine. The relic would not kick over. Blas tried his hand and then Sergeant Dongalio tried his. The engine sat there as stubborn as an Army mule. "Go get that blowtorch from Mama Rosalia, Gary," said Blas. "We got to use desperate measures like it says in the dime novels."

"What dime novels?" asked Gary curiously.

"The Bobbsey Twins!" yelled Blas. "Git!"

Gary got. He was deathly afraid of Mama Rosalia whose feelers were out for gunners from the Navy or artillerymen from the Army to help her reconstruct her double-deadly cannon. Deadly for the enemy *and* the gunners. Papa Alibongbong had been mysteriously missing for three days since she had started to rebuild the cannon.

Gary brought back the blowtorch in double-quick time. Blas lighted it. He heated the manifold, carburetor, and engine. "Kick her over, Mac," he said to Dongalio. The engine coughed and then spluttered. Blas frowned. Eugene chattered angrily. Again and again Blas heated the stubborn engine, and again and again it coughed, spluttered, and died. It was no use.

The sun was slanting to the west when they quit at last. Abundio squatted beside the useless engine. "There is a lovely International, one-cylinder horizontal one-half to two-and-one-half horsepower engine with two flywheels down the mountain," he said.

"Where?" snapped Bob.

Abundio shrugged. "In the Jap outpost on that little island just off the river."

"You think they don't need it?" said Blas.

"We could maybe borrow it," said Gary.

Sergeant Dongalio looked at his weary men. "It is necessary to have this radio operating soon," he said quietly. "The sooner the radio is operating, perhaps the sooner The Aid comes. Is it understood?"

117

Here and there a head nodded.

"General MacArthur is depending upon the men of this *boroba*," said the young sergeant. "It is necessary thus to *be* men. Is it understood?"

A few more heads nodded.

"Without the weather information, the planes cannot find the way. The weather reports must come from *this* radio. Is it understood?"

About half the heads nodded.

Sergeant Dongalio looked at Bob. "We will be back as soon as possible," he said. He turned on a heel and walked down the slope with his tired shoulders squared. He did not look back. One man after another slung his rifle and started after the young noncom. In a little while they were out of sight among the trees of the lower slopes.

"There goes a man," said Blas.

Bob looked at the tough, muscular Regular Navy man. "You ought to know, Blas," he said quietly.

There was nothing more they could do with the broadcast set. There were other things to do. There was little leisure time at a guerrilla base. Lieutenant Phil Kelly was setting up the improvised weather station with the help of Sergeant Jerry Hoffman. Blas, Gary, and Bob gave them a hand. Every bit of weather equipment except a box of weather balloons had been lost or had been taken away by *Grayfin* in her wounded flight from Mindoro. Jerry Hoffman had set up some neatly carved bamboo wind vanes. The officer explained the other gear to his little audience. "We've had to improvise, but that seems to be the motto of the Bamboo Army, lads. We can use a hand anemometer to indicate wind pressure. Jerry has worked out some wind velocity devices as you can see. Not accurate enough for a top-flight weather station, but sufficient enough for us until we can do better. I dug out a

118

good thermometer from a photo kit we salvaged from *Grayfin*. We've got plenty of weather balloons anyway. Trouble is the Jap recon planes will spot 'em. You ever shoot at a balloon in the air?"

Bob nodded. "For some reason they seem impossible to hit."

"Right! I've seen Jap planes dive on 'em, all guns blazing, and nothing happens. They'll get some of them but not *all* of them. One way or another we'll get our information back to Australia."

"If we ever get the radio working," said Gary gloomily.

"What's wrong now?" said the officer.

"First it was the transformer. Then it was the engine. Sergeant Dongalio has gone down to the coast to get a Jap engine."

Kelly looked thoughtfully down the slope. "With only a handful of men, hey?"

"Yes," said Blas.

Kelly fiddled with an improvised instrument. "God run with him," he said.

Jerry Hoffman looked through the instrument used to track the weather balloons. "Looks like a *Chibasco* forming over there, sir," he said.

They all looked down toward Verde Passage and beyond. The sky was turning black. Even as they watched the air seemed to turn warmer and heavier. Kelly eyed the approaching storm. "*Chibasco?*" he said thoughtfully. "No, Hoffman. That's a typhoon or I've never seen one."

No orders were given but Bob, Gary, and Blas raced back to the radio shack. They had gone through too much to lose that all-too-precious radio, paid for by the blood of at least twenty Filipinos. The air had suddenly become very quiet. The dark line against the sky was moving toward northern Mindoro with frightful speed. They took

119

the radio and its heavy table from the hut and lashed the table against a thick-boled tree. They took ropes of abacá fiber and ran them as guys from the radio shack. The air was getting thick and oppressive. They had just finished their lashing when there was an ominous quiet. Bob stole a look over his shoulder and fear got a hold on him. The black line was racing swiftly toward the island with faint, evil-looking light flickering along the face of it, while below it, reaching like a sheet to the waters of Verde Passage was hard driving rain.

There was nothing to do but wait. The sound of the wind changed from a whining to a high-pitched moaning. Leaves began to be stripped from the treetops as the trees swayed in the gale. A limb cracked and hung down, and the wind snapped it off and drove it end over end into the dimness beyond. Bob, Gary, Blas, and Abundio lay down behind a log. A moment later the full smash of the wind struck solidly at the base camp like a living thing. Bob raised his head and ducked it again as a bucket rose off the ground and was hurled right at him. It smashed against a tree behind him and fell clattering to the ground, a flattened mass. The rain came horizontally, stinging like buckshot.

Water began to rise on the soaked ground, driven by the wind into wrinkled sheets. It got deeper and deeper, flowing through the radio shack. The aerial snapped loose, hung streaming like a pennant in the wind, and then vanished into the howling murk. A chicken was whipped up into the air and smashed into a bloody pulp against a galvanized-iron water tank.

A tree wavered. Something cracked, and the tree fell as though sliced through by a gigantic pair of shears. It struck a shack and smashed it flat, and pieces of the shack were driven off through the air. Trees began to burst like

120

fragmentation bombs. Coconuts smashed against the ground or trees, bursting and scattering their milky fluid.

The water rose on the ground until the frightened fugitives behind the log were forced to crawl behind the galvanized-iron tank, which shook on its concrete base. Water leaked through the splitting seams. The guy ropes of the radio shack snapped one by one, and a moment later the shack collapsed like wet cardboard and was scattered by the roaring wind down the slope into the swiftly rising stream. The foot bridge swayed in the liquid grip of the racing water, bent in the middle and parted, breaking the vine lashings that held it to the banks, so that both halves went swirling downstream in the thick and muddy flood.

Eugene chattered wildly, poking his head into Blas's armpit, shivering and twitching as the rain lashed his little body. Blas drew the shaking creature closer to him. "Take it easy, Cousin," he said.

A joint snapped in the metal of the tank. Water spouted from it and was driven straight out by the force of the wind. The tank swayed dangerously. The four fugitives crawled inch by inch through the flood, digging in toes and fingers to gain a hold. Gary fell and was driven down the slope with the muddy water flowing over his face. Blas handed Eugene to Abundio and grabbed Gary, dragging him behind an overturned truck. They all crawled into the body of the truck. The wind-lashed rain struck the bottom of the truck with a sound like that of hail, and the truck swayed a little but seemed firmly enough rooted in the thick and viscous mud beneath the flowing water.

The light was gone. It was like being in a darkened tunnel filled to overflowing with wind and water. One could not talk. It was almost impossible to think. They sat with their heads bowed, bracing their backs against the bed of the truck as though that would keep it from being

121

driven into the raging stream like a toy vehicle. They had no idea where the rest of the guerrillas were or how they were making out. Now and then something snapped or shattered in the madness of wind and rain, but they had no idea of what it was.

Bob thought of the radio. If the typhoon destroyed it, they would be right where they had been before the barrio raid and the deaths and wounds of many guerrillas would have been a useless expenditure. He wondered how Sergeant Dongalio was making out. He would have been caught on the downslope in the howling murk with no protection whatsoever, the trees falling or being driven through the maelstrom like broomstraws. God help them!

Every so often something struck the bottom of the truck with seemingly enough force to come right through and kill or wound the fugitives, but somehow the truck managed to hold off the vicious onslaught of the typhoon.

They had no idea whether it was day or night, or how many hours they had been sheltered in the truck when all at once there was a noticeable lessening of the wind. The rain stopped. The wind veered a little, howled with increased fury and then began to drop steadily in velocity. Several hours went by until at last it had dropped to gale force on the Beaufort Scale, about 41 to 47 miles per hour nautical. Bob dropped off to sleep to waken hours later. The wind had died down to about the velocity of a strong breeze, about 22 to 27 miles per hour nautical.

The sky grew lighter, with a watery effect. The wind turned cold. It wavered back and forth, shifting and varying until at last it was blowing about a moderate breeze. Bob crawled stiffly from the truck and looked about. The place was a shambles. Many huts and shacks had vanished completely. Trees littered the muddy ground that was pocked with many pools of water. The stream was still roaring between its banks carrying great tangles of twisted vines, logs, and branches, with here and there the bodies of animals, birds, and snakes. A tree weakened by the wind and the soaked ground fell slowly, raising a great hummock of muddy earth about the roots.

Blas whistled softly. "All our work for nothing," he said.

"*Bahála ná,*" said Abundio. He examined a gash on his forearm. "There is plenty more bamboo and vines. We can build another base."

"I was thinking about the radio and other gear," said Blas.

Phil Kelly picked his way through the debris. "Blew away the wind cups," he said dryly. "Have to start all over again. Any casualties?"

"We don't know yet," said Bob.

Abundio looked up. "I will check, sir," he said.

Kelly took off his shirt and wrung it out. "It's a great war. One thing about a typhoon, it doesn't choose sides. I hope the Nips got it worse than we did."

"The radio seems all right, Bob!" called out Gary.

"We'll need a shack for it," said Bob.

"No problem," said the officer. "Look."

A file of fuzzy-headed little men were coming out of the dripping jungle. One by one they crossed a log that had providentially fallen across the stream just about where the footbridge had been. As the light grew, the little Mangyans set to work. The sound of their bolos chopping out bamboo and vines echoed through the trees.

In three days the base camp looked much as it had been before the typhoon. The tropical sun had dried the ground. The debris had been hauled off into the jungle. The sound of hammers, files, and hacksaws sounded in place of the raging wind. The BC radio had been set up in an exact replica of the destroyed radio shack. A new aerial wire hung in the highest tree available. Phil Kelly and Jerry Hoffman had reestablished their improvised weather station. There was nothing to do but wait for the engine Dongalio had promised to take from the Japanese and deliver to the radio station.

Three more days had drifted past when a *bojong* sounded through the jungle. Bob looked up from a water-stained radio instruction manual he was studying. "That must be Dongalio with the new engine," he said.

"We *hope* he has the new engine," said Gary.

They walked together toward the head of the trail. A struggling procession moved into sight down the slope. A heavy engine was suspended from carrier poles carried on the shoulders of sixteen almost totally exhausted Filipinos. They carried it to the radio shack and eased it to the ground. Blas quickly looked it over. "Prime," he said. "Dongalio ought to get a medal for this."

Colonel Bledsoe had appeared. "He will," he said, "if I have anything to say about it." He looked at the beat Filipinos. "Where is Sergeant Dongalio?"

Corporal Tomas took off his shapeless straw hat. "We got into the Jap outpost without much trouble, sir," he said quietly. "By the time we got the engine unbolted from its base the Hapons were bringing in a landing barge loaded with Hapon Marines. It was necessary to move fast. There were not enough of us to fight and to get the engine safely into the cover of the jungle." He looked down at the ground.

"Go on, Tomas," said Bledsoe sharply.

Tomas looked up with tears in his brown eyes. "It was necessary to have a rear guard, you understand."

"Sergeant Dongalio?" asked the colonel.

"Yes. There was much shooting but we got away. We hid the engine, and I went back that night to find the

124

sergeant. I found him, sir." Tomas passed a dirty hand across his eyes. "They had finally killed him. They used him for bayonet practice after tying him to a tree. I do not know how long he lived. We would not have escaped if he had not stayed behind, sir."

It was very quiet except for the sighing of the wind through the trees. Colonel Bledsoe took off his hat. "He said something to me once during a bad fight in which we did not think we could escape." He looked about at the men. "It was this: 'Only those who are not afraid to die are fit to live.'" Bledsoe turned on a heel and walked quickly away.

Some of the exhausted Filipinos shuffled their feet. They did not look at each other. Corporal Tomas looked at the engine. "In any case, there is the engine." That was all he had to say. There was no need to say anything further.

Blas watched the Filipinos walk slowly off. "Come on, shipmates," he said. "There's a war on and we need that radio. That would be the way Sergeant Dongalio would have wanted it."

Only those who are not afraid to die are fit to live.

12 . . .

BOB MADE CONTACT with the press key. He adjusted to exact frequency by listening to the receiver and watching the calibration. He switched on the Mindanao station and heard the chatter of their messages coming out. He looked up at the intent face of Colonel Jim Bledsoe. "I can break in on them when they aren't busy, sir," he said.

Bledsoe nodded. He smashed a right fist into his left palm. "Lordy, lordy," he breathed. "I hope we can contact Darwin this time. We've *got* to contact them, Bob."

Bob wiped the sweat from his face as he listened to the Mindanao radio traffic. It had taken four more days to get into operation. The engine that had been paid for by the life of Sergeant Dongalio had been fine. Engine and generator had been doing the job until Blas noted a slight thread of smoke coming out of the transformer. The smoke increased and then really flowed out of it. It had taken a whole day to get the transformer back into business. Luckily the trouble had been in the outer layers of wire. The fused wire had been unwound and repaired, using paper wrapping. Then it was discovered that there wasn't enough gasoline to start the engine. Runners had been sent for more. By the time they returned, with about half a drum, two more days had passed. They had to start the engine on gasoline, for the crude oil they used to operate the engine would keep it running, but could not start it.

Bob looked up at the colonel. "I can try Mindanao now, sir," he said.

Bledsoe nodded. Blas raised his two hands, opened the first two fingers of each hand, placed one pair atop the other and spat accurately through the triangular hole for luck.

Bob broke in. The Mindanao station stopped transmitting, then answered. "How are you receiving us?" queried Bob. The answer was immediate. "QRK5-QRK5." Bob grinned.

"What does that mean?" said Gary.

"Loud and clear signal being received," said Bob. "We're in business as far as Mindanao is concerned."

"¡Bueno!" said Bledsoe. "Now we need Darwin. Two thousand miles, kid. Can we make it?"

Bob shrugged. He patted the top of the set. "She'll make it all right," he said.

"How do you know it's a she?" said Gary.

Bob grinned again. "Kept us guessing a long time before she made up her mind."

"We'll need more crude oil," said Bledsoe.

Mama Rosalia was looking in the window. "There is that Hapon tanker that was sunk offshore, my colonel. Many drums of crude oil are on the beach or in the swamps."

"How many days to get them up here?" said the colonel.

"Three perhaps, my colonel."

"You will take charge?"

The Amazon nodded. She looked down at a fisted hand. "It is said that Papa Alibongbong has joined a fishing

127

crew down that way," she said thoughtfully. "Perhaps he has forgotten his wife."

Blas looked after her as she hurried to round up a party to get the crude oil. "If she catches up with him, he'll *never* forget her," he said.

"Try Darwin," said Bledsoe to Bob.

Bob nodded. This was the acid test. That was why they had struggled so hard to get the radio back from the Japanese and why they had kept on and on after so many heartbreaking setbacks to get it into operation. Nothing could go wrong now. He had the right frequency and the allotted time. "FFTP calling KAZ. FFTP calling KAZ. FFTP calling KAZ." FFTP was Freedom for the Philippines. Frederico Campos had selected that call signal. "FFTP calling KAZ. FFTP calling KAZ."

Two hours later the engine vibrated to a shuddering stop, and while Blas and Abundio worked on it to get it started again Bob and Gary went over the radio with a microscopic examination. They checked the aerial. By the time the engine was running again they were completely bewildered. Why weren't they reaching Australia?

"Check Mindanao to see if they are in contact with Darwin," suggested Blas from the doorway. He wiped the grease and oil from his hands and face.

Bob broke in on Mindanao. Mindanao had just signed off after receiving and transmitting to Darwin. Mindanao was running out of fuel for their engine and would have to remain silent for a few days.

"Ask about the weather between here and Darwin," said Gary.

They had little to report. No reported storms, but at that distance there could be many.

Phil Kelly came into the shack. "Possibility there might be mineral deposits around here interfering?" he asked.

Bob shook his head. "We checked that out the other day."

"Try again," said Gary.

The engine kicked over and the generator went to work. "FFTP calling KAZ. FFTP calling KAZ. FFTP calling KAZ." By the time dusk fell the engine came to a halt. There was no crude oil left.

"Three days until Mama Rosalia gets back," said Gary. He struck the palm of his right hand against his temple. *"Oi vey!"*

The rain started right after dusk and fell straight down with a deadly monotony. Blas and Abundio, with the help of two Mangyans, had built a shelter roof over the engine and generator. Bob had had to shout over to Blas or Abundio to operate the engine, so Gary rigged a signal bell from an old doorbell he had scrounged somewhere out of Papa Alibongbong's scrap boxes. He hooked up the wire with a telegraph key, and by the time the engine shelter had been built, Bob could communicate with the operator by means of the bell.

Blas came dripping in from the outside. "What's the SOP with the signals, Bob?" he asked. He picked up Eugene and placed him on one of his shoulders.

"One bell to start. Two to stop. Three to reduce power. Four to increase power. Five, forget the whole business and go to chow."

"That's the best part of it," said Gary, "that No. 5."

Blas nodded. "Well, we've got everything ready to go except Darwin," he said. "You don't suppose they quit the war and went home, do you?"

"Mindanao talked to them this afternoon," said Gary.

"Yeh," said Blas. "This is what they call an impossible, isn't it, Bob?"

"Imponderable," said Bob. Blas had hit it on the head.

Everything was right. Nothing could be wrong. And yet no Darwin.

The rain pattered steadily on the roof and dripped from the eaves. Blas and Gary went off to chow. Bob stayed at the set, trying to figure things out. He hauled out the manual and reread it for about the fifth time, trying to find something he might have missed, but it was no use. There was no use in trying Mindanao again. They were off the air.

Colonel Bledsoe came in. "No luck at all?"

Bob shook his head. "Nothing, sir."

"Beats me." Bledsoe shook the rain from his woven hat. "The Bamboo Telegraph claims there's something big for us on the minds of the boys at GHQ-SWPA."

"What do you think, sir?"

Bledsoe looked thoughtfully at Bob. "I think it's The Aid at last, Bob."

"Invasion!" said Bob.

Bledsoe nodded his head. "Not right away, Mac. There are preliminaries, and I think that's going to be our job. To pave the way for the boys when they get here. Can't take any chances. Things have to be ready and right for them. A war could very well be lost otherwise."

Bob slapped the top of the stubborn set.

"Go get some chow. Mama Rosalia made it before she left."

"I waste no time!" said Bob. "Who cooks while she's gone?"

Bledsoe looked casual. "Your shipmate," he said.

"Blas is the best cook in the Navy," said Bob.

"Not him," said the officer. "The *other* one. We need Blas on the engine."

Bob shook his head. "Well, there are always bananas," he said resignedly.

130

Blas and Gary were still in the improvised mess hall when Bob dripped in and sat down. "What is it tonight?" said Bob. "Spam and beans? *Kuru* bark?" He looked fixedly at Eugene. "Monkey stew?"

Eugene leaped for cover. Blas scowled at Bob. "Cannibal," he growled.

"Roasted-rice coffee," said Gary, ticking off on his fingers. "*Poto sicle*—baked rice bread. *Pechay*—lettuce cabbage. *Adobo!* That's spiced barbecue of chicken and pork with brown rice. Jungle plant salad. Dessert is thin-sliced coconut in tart fruit juice and brown sugar."

"Yeh, yeh," said Bob.

"It's true!" said Gary.

"What's for breakfast?" said Bob.

Eugene scampered for cover under the eyes of Bob and Gary. "Fried *kuru* bark," said Gary. "You'll love it!"

Mama Rosalia *had* prepared roasted-rice coffee, *pechay*, *adobo*, *poto sicle*, and coconut dessert. Bob ate the last scrap and nodded in satisfaction. "Happy birthday," he said to himself.

"Your birthday isn't until January," said Gary.

"Happy birthday anyway," said Bob.

"You get the radio going, kid?" said Blas.

Bob shook his head. "Jungle Jim says the Bamboo Telegraph claims there's something big going on for us in the minds of the characters at GHQ-SWPA."

"Such as?" said Blas. He refilled the coffee cups with the roasted-rice coffee.

"The Aid," said Bob.

"No!" said Gary.

Bob sipped his coffee. "There are preliminaries," he said. "Jungle Jim says that's to be our job."

"Well, I'll be cooking," said Gary quickly.

"Mama Rosalia will be back in three days," said Bob.

131

There was a sickly grin on Gary's face. "You'll need her for the cannon!"

Blas looked at his grease-blackened fingernails as though he had never seen them before. "She'll need help on the cannon now that Papa Alibongbong is doing his bit by fishing for his country."

Bob nodded wisely. "Like a gunner's mate third class, eh, Blas?"

Blas rubbed his stubbly jaw. "Exactly."

"You wouldn't dare," said Gary.

"Try us," said Bob with a broad and confident smile.

Gary vanished into the wet and dripping night.

"You don't suppose he'd *buqwee?*" asked Blas thoughtfully.

Bob grinned. "After seeing that crazy cannon peel like a banana I wouldn't blame anyone for *buqweeing,* and you know if Mama Rosalia ever finds out about Gary, she'll never stop until she gets him on that gun crew. It'd be like a Greek tragedy, Blas. The end would be inevitable."

Blas swirled his coffee around in his cup. "The Aid," he said. He looked up at the ceiling.

"What do you think we might have to do, Blas?"

The cook shrugged. "The Japs have minefields in these channels. Our Navy won't know where they are. We already know we have to send weather information so our planes will know when the right conditions are here. The army will want to know about their fortifications. Troop concentrations and suchlike. Lots of things, Mac. I have a sneaking suspicion we're going to be more than busy before we get back aboard the ol' *Grayfin.*"

"You think we will, Blas?"

Blas held out a hand to Eugene and swung him up onto his shoulder. "I'm betting on it," he said.

They walked through the steady drizzle to the radio

shack and lighted a few *kinkie* lamps, fueled by coconut oil. In the soft, flickering yellow light, Bob pored over the manual again while Blas unrolled the banigs, or woven sleeping mats, they used.

Bob looked up after a time. "It's no use," he said. "I think we're beat, Blas."

"Don't ever say that, Bob." There wasn't much confidence in the big cook's voice. Blas placed Eugene on his own sleeping mat behind the radio table. "How about a game of cards to kill the time?"

Bob shook his head. "Let me try the receiver on something else." He switched it on and picked up a singsong language they could not identify. They caught a faint, almost indistinguishable broadcast from Radio Chungking. A voice with an unmistakable Japanese accent spoke in English from some other source, the usual propaganda.

"I'd rather listen to Tokyo Rose," said Blas as he lay down. "At least *she* plays good music. All this character does is talk and brag, and with an Oxford accent yet!"

Later Bob lay looking up at the dark ceiling of the hut. Gary came in and unrolled his banigs and dropped on them. "We're getting low on supplies again," said he. "We might end up with fried *kuru* bark yet. Any luck, Mac?"

"No," said Bob.

"Useless, hey?"

"I'm beginning to think so."

Gary nodded. "I think so too."

They dropped asleep listening to the steady pattering of the rain on the thatch. It would likely rain all night and through the next day. Mama Rosalia and her crew would have a time hauling the heavy fuel-oil drums up the greasy slopes, and when they got there, they would find out they might just as well have left the drums washing about in the oily surf. FFTP was completely out of business.

133

13 . . .

BLAS KICKED OVER the old International. She coughed, rattled, spluttered, and wheezed and then after a few hitches and hesitations, she settled down into a steady pounding. The whole *boroba* had gathered to see the operation, and for once Jungle Jim Bledsoe didn't tongue-lash them back to their jobs. It was important to them all to contact Australia, for was that not where The Aid would come from? Was that not where General MacArthur commanded? Was it not he who would bring The Aid back to the Philippines?

Bob looked up at the taut face of the colonel and nodded. "All set," he said. "FFTP calling KAZ. FFTP calling KAZ." Twenty minutes drifting past did not help anyone's nerves with the constant: "FFTP calling KAZ. FFTP calling KAZ."

The receiver hummed for a moment. It stopped humming, then hummed again and faintly they heard the voice. "KAZ calling FFTP." It was hardly distinguishable and suddenly it stopped short.

Pandemonium broke loose. Straw hats sailed up into the air. Filipinos danced wildly about and Americans, in their more gentle way, pounded each other mercilessly on the back. Bob frowned. Why had the reception cut off like that? "FFTP calling KAZ. FFTP calling KAZ. Come in please. FFTP calling KAZ. Our reception very poor. FFTP calling KAZ."

Minutes ticked past. Then faintly came the sound of the operator at the other end. "KAZ calling . . ." It broke off. Bob wiped the sweat from his face. Everyone was very quiet now. "FFTP calling KAZ. FFTP calling KAZ. Come in please. Reception is very bad. Broken off. FFTP calling KAZ. How do you receive me? Come in please. FFTP calling KAZ."

An hour later the Filipinos were quietly back at work, looking up now and then at the radio shack. The engine still thudded along, echoing through the trees, but there was still no noise from the shack. The Aid seemed just as far away as ever.

Gary took over from Bob. Bob's voice was wearing out. "FFTP calling KAZ. FFTP calling KAZ. Come in please," repeated Gary over and over again. He would not look at Bob or Blas. He did not want to see what was in their eyes, nor did they want to see the gathering hopelessness in his. Even little Eugene was quiet and subdued. He crawled off to his miniature banig for his siesta.

Gary patted the set on the top. "Come on, you big overgrown tin can!" he pleaded. "Give, baby, give!"

The receiver broke into ragged life. "KAZ calling FFTP. We received you loud and clear. No seeming problem at this end. We received you loud and clear. QRK5. QRK5. QRK5." Then it seemed to snap off into silence.

Bob had opened his mouth to yell. He closed it.

Gary was at it again with sweat running down his tense face. "FFTP calling KAZ. QRK5. QRK5." Silence. "Try again please. FFTP calling KAZ."

"This is crazy," said Blas. "There's no sense to it. No sense at all."

Bob sat down on a bamboo stool, staring at the set and the receiver, trying to concentrate. Supposing he *had* done something wrong? He wasn't a radioman, but that wasn't any excuse. A Bamboo Warrior had to adapt himself to all kinds of situations and emergencies.

The receiver hummed. "QRK5. QRK5." It shut off for a moment and then flicked into life again. "KAZ calling FFTP. QRK5." Then silence again.

Bob rubbed his jaw. He looked at the receiver and at the wire that trailed below it. There was a thicker wire hanging there and as he looked at it, *it moved!* Bob got to his feet. The thicker wire vanished.

"—FFTP. KAZ calling FFTP. KAZ call—"

Bob looked under the heavy table. Eugene wasn't sleeping peacefully on his miniature banig. He was chewing away at the wire that led into the receiver. The wire had already been partially severed, and the connection at the other end was loose in its socket, wobbling back and forth as Eugene chewed away industriously. Even as Bob watched the receiver broke into life. "Check your receiving apparatus, FFTP. Check your—"

"*EUGENE!*" howled Bob. "He wasn't sleeping at all! He's been chewing the wires! He's been doing it off and on for *days! AAAARGH!*" Bob dived for the monkey. Eugene headed for a far corner, and one of Gary's unlaced jungle boots thudded into the wall just over his head.

"Murderers!" yelled Blas. He dived for Gary. Gary went under Blas's thick outstretched arms and hurled his other boot at Eugene. The boot hit Bob at the back of the head, half stunning him. He fell over the stool and hit a leg of the table. The table wobbled a little. Blas had missed Gary. He fell over the table. The receiver fell to the floor, missing Eugene by an inch. Gary picked up his chair and chased Eugene into a corner, but the monkey was too fast for Gary. He jumped between Gary's legs full into Bob's arms. Bob grabbed at thin air and received a sharp nip on

136

the thumb as Eugene headed for the door. Blas tried to get up, but the table slowly collapsed, hitting the rear wall, which sagged perilously. As Gary raced past trying to reach Eugene, Blas thrust out a thick leg. Gary went headfirst into the front wall. The bamboo support had been loosened by the rain and the whole shack sagged that way. Bob jumped over Blas and fell over Gary. As he hit the wall with his shoulder the whole roof slid sideways and collapsed atop the radio set and the three struggling occupants of the shack. A black streak raced past Colonel Bledsoe, leaping for a trailing vine with outstretched arms, and in a few seconds Eugene had returned to his native element.

The Filipinos who dragged the three *Grayfin* men from the wreckage were convulsed with laughter. Now and then one of them would slap his thighs or roll helplessly on the ground.

Gary, Bob, and Blas sat on the ground looking glumly at the hilarious guerrillas. Even Jungle Jim Bledsoe had a smile on his tanned face. Bob looked at Blas. Blas wiped his bloody nose. Gary fingered a lump on his shaved head. Bob sucked at his perforated thumb.

From under the wreckage came the clear sound of the KAZ operator. "KAZ calling FFTP. What is wrong? We were receiving you loud and clear. What is wrong? KAZ calling FFTP. What is wrong?"

Bob glanced at Blas. The big cook had been ready to kill because of his beloved cousin Eugene. Blas looked gloweringly at Bob. "They want to know what's wrong, Mac," he said. "If we *told* them, do you think they'd ever believe that *my* cousin Eugene bollixed up the works?"

After that sally, there was nothing else to do but reerect the collapsed shack and set up the radio again between bouts of hysterical laughter when most of the willing crew were totally incapacitated. Bob remembered that Eugene had had a habit of vanishing under the radio table to his banig just about the time the receiver would start its mysterious gyrations. Now he knew the *real* meaning behind "monkey business."

That evening Bob transmitted the piled-up code messages and received a number of them, also in code, from KAZ—messages that had originated from GHQ-SWPA. Phil Kelly and the colonel decoded the messages.

The next day the colonel passed the information on to the assembled *boroba*. "We have our work to do, men. It has been outlined for us. It's up to us to fill in the details and get the jobs done. It won't be easy. But the sooner we get started and get them done, the sooner The Aid will come."

"What is it they want, my colonel?" asked Mama Rosalia.

"I'm glad you asked," said the colonel with a wry smile. "They want plotted channels through the minefields in Verde Passage. They want coast watchers and observers to check on all passing Jap ships, naval and merchant marine going through the passage. They want an accurate check on them for types, tonnage, etc. They want to know the numbers and calibers of guns on the islands out there and the numbers of troops as well. They want to know about air traffic. Directions, numbers of planes, types of planes, possible air routes. They want constant weather reports. *This is extremely important.* That's your department, Phil. We are to receive relayed radio reports from the Manila Bay area on air bases, air activities, antiaircraft gun emplacements, troop and supply data. We will have to prepare maps here for that purpose and insert the information as we receive it from their mobile radio stations. *It must be absolutely accurate!* They stressed that again and again. Ammo dumps, camouflaged airplane run-

138

ways, fuel dumps, plane revetments, food stockpiles, searchlights, shelters, lookout posts, ship-repair docks, docks, and loading facilities, *every potential air target around Manila Bay and in Verde Passage.* This last will be our personal job. The rest will be relayed to us as I have said. We are to receive top-secret written reports from Manila, southern Luzon, Maricaban, Marinduque, Lubang and Ambil Islands and we are to deliver them to a submarine rendezvous for delivery to GHQ-SWPA. They would take up too much time to be transmitted by radio. If those reports are ever captured by the Hapons, many people will die, for their names are mentioned in those reports. Names that are necessary for GHQ to know.

"We are to receive a number of 88 radios for short-range intercommunication on this island. Powerful field glasses have been sent to us from Australia along with the 88's—in short, everything we need to do this job except guts. We'll have to supply *that* ourselves." Bledsoe looked from one to another of his command. "Any questions?" he added.

"We do not have many men," said Corporal Tomas.

"We will be joined by two more *borobas*," said Bledsoe. "There are a number of Bolo Battalions along the coast we can also use."

"Perhaps we will need more artillery," said Mama Rosalia.

"The best I can do is line up a few bazookas. They'll have to do."

"Could you find me a gunner?" asked Mama Rosalia.

Bledsoe's gray eyes flicked at Gary. Gary paled beneath his tan. He furtively eyed the vines by which Eugene had made good his escape into the jungle. A fellow might not be as good at it as cousin Eugene, but he could *try.*

"No," said Bledsoe. "You'll have to get along without one, Mama Rosalia, unless you find Papa Alibongbong."

"That son of a pig," she said. "If I ever catch him I . . ." Her voice trailed off in her anger.

"We'll have to get observers out on those islands where the Hapons have the guns," said Abundio.

"Volunteers," said Bledsoe. "We'll need radio operators for that."

Gary paled. "I was just thinking about finding a gunner for Mama Rosalia," he said.

Bledsoe shook his head. "Radio operators are more important. Bob, you'll have to do a little teaching on radio operation."

Bob smiled wanly. "I wish someone would teach *me*," he said.

"We'll have to get our gear down to the coast. Establish coast watcher and mobile radio stations, set up outposts to guard the coast watchers and radio stations. We will need bancas to get out to the islands. The Mangyans can be used to set up a spy system to relay Hapon movements to our Bolo Battalions. I have information that the Hapons are reinforcing their troops on this island, but not with third-raters like the Formosans and Koreans. Imperial Marines, my friends, and you know what that means."

Bob felt cold inside. He had run into those tough babies before. They were thoroughly dedicated. The Samurai of the Imperial forces, and equally as dedicated and tough as the United States Marines. Furthermore, to die for the Emperor was their main ambition.

"They have doubled their patrol boats in Verde Passage. Then too, we might have the Q-boats to deal with."

"Q-boats, sir?" said Jerry Hoffman. "What are they?"

Bledsoe shrugged. "*¿Quién sabe?* They are supposed to be concentrating in Balayan Bay, Batangas Bay at Tabangao, Janao Bay near Anilao, and between **Mabini and Bauan**, all on Verde Passage. We have no information on them except that the Hapons supposedly place a great deal of reliance on them to deal with our ships. I don't like the smell of them, but there isn't much we can do about it, other than find out what they are and what they can do. We can fit them in somewhere, I suppose." He grinned. "Any more questions?" No one spoke. "*Sigi legi, ho!*" he added. "*Alibongbong!*"

Bob didn't have much else to do but stick with the radio, but he could hear the activity going on in the hidden base all around him. Bledsoe had everything organized, but the numbers of his force were few indeed and poorly armed, even with the addition of two more *borobas*, the Bolo Battalions and the loyal help of the Mangyans. Imperial Marines . . . the thought left him uneasy.

They would have to move the entire operation down to the coastline, within easy reach of Japanese patrol boats and planes, as well as probing landing parties. The Japanese would know that the guerrillas would have increased activities. They weren't fools. They would know an invasion was contemplated. "Q-boats," he said aloud.

Gary looked up from the spare parts box he was packing. "That bothering you too?" he said.

"They had Q-ships in World War I," said Bob. "My uncle told me about them."

"What'd they do? What were they like?"

"Merchant ships. They were fitted to stay afloat as long as possible by being loaded with barrels and lumber. Naval guns were concealed on them behind steel doors that could drop down so they could open fire in a matter of seconds. The idea was to send them out into submarine-infested areas, acting like innocent merchant ships. When

141

the sub appeared, the crew would panic. They'd blow off steam and so on. Then the crew seemingly would abandon the ship."

"Who fired the guns?"

"The gun crews would stay aboard. The sub might cruise in close and examine the ship. They didn't like to waste torpedoes, preferring to sink a ship by shellfire if possible. It took a lot of nerve to wait behind those screens watching a U-boat coming closer and closer until she was within range."

"They ever get any U-boats?"

Bob nodded. "Quite a few I guess. I don't really know how many."

"You think the Japs might have something like that?"

"It doesn't seem likely."

"Then what are they?"

Bob shrugged. " '¿Quién sabe?' like the colonel says."

"Yeh," said Gary thoughtfully.

"Where's Blas?"

"Looking for cousin Eugene."

"In the dark?"

Gary nodded. "He's afraid we might have to leave and Eugene won't be able to find his way back before we go." He looked at Bob. "I know what you're thinking."

"We couldn't be *that* lucky." Bob laughed.

Later that night, when Bob and Gary were asleep on their banigs, and Blas lay awake staring up at the roof of the shack, a little black figure dropped from a tree, scurried across the clearing and peered into the shack. It dropped soundlessly inside and crept across the floor to Blas. Blas raised an arm and the little figure nestled within it. Cousin Eugene *had* been able to find his way back before they left.

14 . . .

THE RAIN had started in five minutes after the guerrillas abandoned their base camp. In half an hour the steep trails were running inches deep in muddy water, and the streams were rising rapidly. By the time they reached the lower ground they were splashing through ankle-deep water and tripping over the vines that floated free of the ground but were entangled and still fastened to the trees from which they had fallen. They were like trip wires, and every now and then a bearer would go down and the pole-slung burdens would swing heavily back and forth, almost throwing the other bearers off-balance. Radios, tools, supplies of every sort, had been packed and covered with tightly woven straw matting for protection, and every ounce of it had to be carried by manpower, for the carabaos could not get down the treacherous slopes, and besides, there were not many of them left. There were plenty of bearers, for the two reinforcing *borobas* had come into the camp the night before, but there was room for only so many bearers on the poles. The going was bad enough in dry weather. In wet weather it was far more treacherous.

The ground was a sticky, gummy mass beneath the racing brown water, and great gobbets of the mud would stick to the bare feet of the bearers until it was almost impossible to walk on until it was scraped off. It was useless to wear shoes and boots, for the mud would suck them off. The useless footwear hung by the laces from the necks of the guerrillas as they worked their tortuous way down the hill slopes toward the swamps and jungles of the lower ground.

The lower ground had razor-edged cogongrass that raked at arms and legs, drawing blood, and even in the rain the *anas* arrived, drawn by the smell of the fresh blood. The leeches appeared out of nowhere to cling and dig in, and the victim could not feel them until they became so swollen with blood that they would hang like great grapes from the flesh. The water was deeper on the lower ground, swirling through the grass and trees, carrying debris of all sorts. At times it was almost impossible to detect streams, for they were all out of their banks and oftentimes the leading bearers would blunder into them and go out of sight in the deeper water, gripped by the swift current. Three men were lost that way their first day on the lower ground.

They reached the little flotilla of barotos and *caba-cabas* that had been hidden for their use and wisely lashed to nearby trees so they would not float off. Even as the men loaded the small boats it was necessary to bail the rainwater out with the *bagools*. The weight of the cargoes and men placed the boats dangerously low in the water. There would be no margin for error. One mistake and a boat would capsize or fill and sink. They had only to steer the boats from the smaller stream into the roaring river, for the current was swift enough to move them without paddling, but it made the steering more difficult. They shot the swollen, muddy waters, with vines and leaves lashing their heads and upper bodies while the rain sluiced down until it seemed as though they were traveling in the bottom of a great tank of water where only passing fish were missing. Now and then logs drove through the water and thudded against the sides of the low-lying boats or shot up out of the water, endangering the men. One guerrilla suffered a broken arm from such a blow. There were times when they had to belly down in the boats because of overhanging branches or entangling skeins of thick, tough lianas. More than once a boat had to be freed of these tangles by desperate bolo-slashing while the boat was slowly tilted down to the swamping point. Then the *bagools* would go into play before the baroto or *caba-caba* went under the muddy water.

"Rain, rain, go away," chanted Gary. He winced as a vine slapped his disreputable straw hat from his head and welted his cheek.

Bob desperately dug in his paddle to turn the baroto away from a slime-covered log that protruded into the stream from the flooded bank. The baroto struck hard and slithered along the log while bare feet were pushed against it to fend it off. The boat swirled past the end of the log into the deep eddy and turned sideways. A *caba-caba* struck the log full on and then began to go over. Only swift work by its crew saved the *caba-caba*. They turned it toward the log and gripped the log, their clutching fingers sliding on the slimy surface. Some of them bellied out onto the log and held the small boat with their feet until it could be bailed out and then they got gingerly back into it again to shove off and enter the mad race down the roaring stream. It was like a mad Tunnel of Love, thought Bob, with a few Mindoro touches.

Blas dug in his paddle and hung onto Eugene with his free hand. "I never thought the day would come when I wished I had joined the Army," he said.

145

"You mean Marines, don't you, Blas?" said Gary.

Blas was horrified. "*Marines?* You crazy! I oughta wash your mouth out with soap and water!"

Gary winked at Bob. He lost his paddle in the churning water and grabbed for it, going neatly over the side into the racing water. He bobbed up in time to be hauled into the colonel's big baroto. He waved cheerfully, grabbed a free paddle and got to work as though nothing had happened.

"That crazy kid," said Blas. He shook his head.

Bob looked away. He had seen the look on the big cook's face when Gary had gone overboard. It was the same look he had had when he had tried to defend Eugene against the onslaught of Bob and Gary.

The river widened. Mangrove swamps appeared on either hand, with their slimy aerial roots providing additional hazards to the fleet of boats plunging down the river toward the distant sea. Their progress was halted by the dusk, for it was far too dangerous to risk the river during darkness. They moored the craft to the mangroves. There was no choice but to stay in the boats, sitting, lying, or squatting in the bilge water. *Bagools* scraped steadily all through the night as the rainwater poured down through the leaves overhead. Balls of cold rice were passed from boat to boat by Mama Rosalia. It was all they had to eat. There was no protection from the rain except the banigs they had brought along. Rude shelters were improvised to keep off the overhead water, but there was no way of escaping the water that rose steadily in the bottoms of the boats—it had to be bailed out before the boat swamped.

The hours dragged past until it seemed as though they had somehow drifted right out of the known world into some vast, primeval land of mud and water, not even inhabited by the great lizards of antediluvian times. Bob

146

wondered if there really was land beyond the stinking, water-deluged mangrove swamp—a land where the sun shone and it was dry. To be dry seemed to be his only ambition. He had even forgotten about food and sleep. Just to be dry!

There was no use in griping. No one spoke. There was nothing to speak about. The rain drove all thoughts out of a man's head, leaving nothing but the primeval instinct to be warm and dry. That was all that mattered.

The sharp-pitched bamboo flute awoke Bob. He tried to sit up and groaned as he felt his stiffened neck. He could not straighten it. The rain had stopped during the night. He shivered in the cold light of the false dawn. Blas reached over and worked tenderly at Bob's neck until he could move it a little and then the big cook snapped it into position.

Jim Bledsoe stood up in his big boat and looked about. Satisfied, he waved on a baroto that had three Filipinos and two Mangyans in it. They would precede the fleet down the river toward the tidal area. Japanese patrol boats could move close into the river mouth.

The sun was high up when at last Bob saw something sparkling far ahead of them. It took him a moment or two to realize it must be the open sea with the bright sun reflecting from the choppy waves. Little sun penetrated the dismal swamp and Bob had a consuming desire to paddle down to a white beach beneath that brilliant sun and let its healing rays soak into his wrinkled flesh and aching bones.

The scout boat had halted. A *bojong* blew three times, and the fleet swung into the mangroves from the channel, forcing their way past the naked, slimy roots until they were out of sight of the river mouth, but they could see the scout boat moving into cover.

Jim Bledsoe took his field glasses from their scarred leather case. He wiped the lens and focused the glasses on the river mouth. Something was moving out there. "*Chidori*-class torpedo boat," he said. "Heavily armed. She's scarcely got steerageway on her."

Half an hour dragged past until the torpedo boat moved out of sight. They had barely paddled the boats out into the channel when they heard the intermittent humming of an engine. They swung back toward the trees and paddled desperately, just getting under cover when a single float plane zoomed low over the river, with the sun flashing from its sides. The red meatball was plainly seen on the sides of the fuselage and on the underside of the wings.

"A Rufe," said Bob. "Float-type Zero."

The plane continued on out into the channel and then banked to fly out of sight. The boats were paddled back out into the river. Bob almost wished for the concealing rain. He changed his mind when the sun hit his wet clothing and the steam arose from them. In less than half an hour he was comparatively dry. They paddled up a side channel deep into the swamp until they reached a rude wharf, half sunken in the flooded waters. There were at least fifty men from a coastal Bolo Battalion waiting for them. The boats were unloaded and the Bolo Battalion boys did most of the carrying. The men of Bledsoe's command were almost dead beat as they sloshed through sticky mud and smelly water to reach a trail that led up out of the mangroves to higher ground. By midafternoon they were traversing low hills, but now and then they had to scatter into the undergrowths as reconnaissance planes swung idly overhead.

They camped that night high on a hill, and containers of hot rice and other food were hauled in from a barrio down the coast. Bob could hardly eat the rich food. His stomach tried to throw it up, but somehow he managed to keep it down. He slept as though it was the next thing to death.

In the morning things seemed better. The guerrillas ate voraciously. They bathed in a clear pool and got rid of their filthy, worn-out garments. They cleaned their gummed-up, rust-flecked weapons and sharpened their bolos. A wizened little Filipino spent the whole day cobbling boots with soles made from old automobile tires.

Jungle Jim Bledsoe had vanished at dawn with a picked crew of guerrillas and guides from the Bolo Battalion. He reappeared at dusk. For an hour his orders crackled out, and parties of guerrillas and bolo men parted company with their units and vanished into the jungle or headed for the long and lonely beaches.

Bob checked out one of the short-range 88-type radios while Gary and Blas checked out a set of walkie-talkies. The moon arose and filled the night with a silvery-looking light while the distant hills seemed frosted with the illumination. Abundio brought additional gear. There were Colt .45 issue automatics and new .30 caliber carbines plus a razor-edged bolo for each man.

Gary eyed the weapons. "We going somewhere, Abundio?" he asked.

The boy nodded. "Corporal Tomas says there is a boat being readied for us."

"To go out there?" Gary jerked a thumb over his shoulder.

Abundio nodded again. "Verde Passage," he said. "There is an island out there. It is said we need a coast watcher out there."

"No idea who it is?" said Gary.

Abundio looked thoughtfully at the 88 set and the walkie-talkies. "There are not many operators of such equipment in our *boroba*," he said.

"There are none," said Gary quickly, "except me and

149

Bob here, and Blas, if he ever gets it through his thick skull."

Abundio smiled and held out his hands, palms upward. "Then it is simple, is it not? It is you and Roberto who must go."

Bob did not look up. His mouth had a sudden brassy taste. Why did it have to be him? He had done more than his share of duty in this crazy war and enough in the Philippines.

"Somebody has to do it," said Blas.

Bob looked at Gary. A message flashed between them. They had both been thinking the same thing. Leave it to Blas to know that. Blas would go of course. It wouldn't be like him to leave his two shipmates.

"There is a banca down at the beach," said Abundio. "They are waiting for us and Mama Rosalia."

"She going too?" said Gary.

Abundio smiled. "She is one of the best banca men, I mean woman, we have. Besides, if the Japs see us, they will not think guerrillas would have a woman in the boat."

"Yeh," said Gary. "I'll bet. They're suspicious of anything and everything, them Hapons."

They lugged their gear down the tangled slopes and into the great coconut groves that lay between the slopes and the beaches. The air was sweet and cool with a plant smell to it. There was a silvery swarming of moonbeams coming down between the tall, graceful coconut palms, whose smooth gray-green trunks had been curved by years of winds blowing in from the sea.

The banca had been run into a narrow inlet, and the mast had been taken down. It was far enough in from the beach that it could not be seen by prowling Japanese patrol boats. They loaded the 88, the walkie-talkies, a barrel of fuel for the small engine to run the generator, a demijohn of lubricating oil, a battery charger and four batteries, the receiver, speaker, transmitter, and spare parts. A Filipino brought down three pairs of binoculars, an alarm clock, and an Army compass with a pelorus arrangement. "I am Fermin Donayre," he said quietly. "Once I was a pilot in these waters. I have served in the United States Navy as a boy."

"Mess boy?" said Blas.

"That is so. But then I *was* a boy. Since that time I have commanded my own craft in these waters and have been a pilot. I am to go with you."

Blas picked a splinter out of his hand. "Why?" he asked.

Fermin looked startled. "It is said that one must plot the channels through the minefields. That is to be my duty on this detail."

"Plot *minefields?*" said Gary faintly. He smiled weakly. "Out *there?*" He jerked a thumb over his shoulder.

"How else does one plot a minefield?" said Fermin in surprise.

"In a banca?" said Blas.

Fermin shook his head. "From an island. The Hapons do not stay on it. They patrol it several times a week. It is only six miles long and a half mile wide, therefore it is necessary for one to be cautious. Is that not so?"

Gary smiled weakly again. "That is so. How far is this island?"

"On the other side of the passage, my friend."

"That's Luzon!" said Bob sharply.

Fermin shrugged. "We must go where the minefields are, must we not?"

"We must indeed," said Bob.

Fermin nodded. "It is necessary to sail after darkness this night. Before dawn we will hide on a small uninhabited island. With luck we can be there in several days."

He shrugged again. "If we could go straight across, we could be there by dawn, but that is not possible. There are too many Hapon patrol boats out there, as well as their planes, so therefore we must go in a roundabout manner."

There was a wild burst of Tagalog in the shadows. Mama Rosalia appeared with Phil Kelly and at a distance lurked the small figure of Papa Alibongbong, who was watching his enraged wife with a wily eye, ready to take off in a flash. He could always outrun Mama Rosalia if he got a twenty-foot head start.

Mama Rosalia stopped beside the banca. "Do not let him in the boat, my captain," she said. "For I will surely drown him! I did not know we would take *his* banca!"

Phil Kelly could not keep a straight face. "It is *The Banca*," he said. "Therefore, as captain and owner, Papa Alibongbong *must* go."

She looked fiercely at her cowering spouse. "I will not promise!" she shouted.

"Then you will not go," said the officer.

She stared at him. "Me? Not go! But this is impossible! *I* will command the banca."

Phil pointed back through the grove. "Your promise or you do not go," he said.

She stood there with glowering brows. She looked at Papa Alibongbong. He got ready to take off. "All right," she said at last. She looked at Bob. "Here! Catch these! I go to get my new cannon." She tossed Bob a couple of pieces of Shelby tubing.

"No!" said Gary. "Not that crazy mixed-up piece of pipe!"

She shook her head. "Wait and see," she said. She vanished into the shadows.

Papa Alibongbong came down to the banca. He sighed.

152

"It was a happy time until she appeared," he said wistfully.

"You are The Captain," said Blas. "You give all the orders. If she doesn't obey or threatens you, you can put her in irons."

The little man looked uncertainly at Blas. "You are sure of this?"

"Positive!"

Papa Alibongbong grew at least an inch. "Then I will tell her so! That is good news!"

The Amazon reappeared, striding easily through the grove, balancing a slightly beat up bazooka on her broad shoulder and carrying a box of ammunition for it in her free hand. "Is this not a beauty?" she called out. She came to the banca, ignoring her husband, and loaded the bazooka and ammunition into the boat.

"Woman!" said Papa Alibongbong in his most commanding tone.

She turned and looked at him in astonishment. "What do you want, little man?"

He drew himself up. "It is said that I am The Captain, and therefore, if my orders are not obeyed by you or you threaten me, you will be put in irons at my command. Do you understand?"

There was a long moment of silence. Bob thought uneasily of getting a twenty-foot start on Mama Alibongbong.

Mama Alibongbong gave a final pat to her beloved bazooka.

"Do you understand?" sternly demanded Papa Alibongbong.

She turned with a sweet and tender smile. "Certainly, Papa," she said softly. "But *who* will put me in the irons you speak of?"

There was a longer silence. Phil Kelly cleared his throat. "The moon is almost gone," he said. He looked at Bob,

153

Gary, and Blas. "I wish I could go with you, but I'm detailed to run the weather station and the radio station at the same time. I'll be hearing from you in a few days, hey?"

They all nodded. The far side of Verde Passage. Patrolled by Japanese planes, submarines, and surface craft. Islands garrisoned by Imperial Marines. Minefields to chart under the noses of those same Imperial Marines.

"How big did you say that island was?" Gary asked Fermin.

"Six miles long and half a mile wide," said the pilot.

"How does one hide on such a sliver in the sea?" said Gary.

"Probably no place to hide," said Blas quietly. "You run until your hat floats."

A hamlike hand caught the big cook between the shoulder blades, staggering him. Mama Rosalia roared with laughter as she slapped her thighs. "You're a riot, kiddo!" she spluttered.

"Yeh," said Blas between set teeth. He closed a rocklike fist and looked longingly at it.

When the moon was almost gone, they waded down the inlet, pulling the heavy banca along with them until they reached the beach. They swung in and paddled out beyond the swell of the surf. They raised the mast and then the triangular sail. Papa Alibongbong took the tiller. The banca skimmed along like a thing alive through the gathering darkness. Bob looked back at Papa Alibongbong. The little man was no longer meek and mild looking. He handled the swiftly moving craft with skill and surety. He was in his element.

Gary looked at Bob. He pointed out into the windy darkness of the passage. *"Bahála ná!"* he said. He dropped into the bottom of the boat and promptly fell asleep.

15 . . .

THE WIND died away completely at midnight, and the banca tossed uneasily on the dark waters. The stars winked down from the cloudless sky overhead, but to the northeast dark clouds blanked out the sky and the stars. The water lapped and gurgled alongside the banca in an oily sort of a swell that did not break. As the banca rose high on a wave Bob could see faint lights far in the distance but he had no idea whether they were on Mindoro or an island or perhaps a Japanese patrol boat. It wouldn't be easy to see the banca in the darkness, but if the wind did not pick up, they would not be able to paddle to an island before the coming of the dawn.

Papa Alibongbong searched the sky. He looked at the cloud bank and shook his head. "It does not look good," he said. "No wind. Thick clouds. It is bad."

"Without a wind it will be worse," said Mama Rosalia.

"Maybe we ought to start paddling," said Blas.

"We could not reach land before the dawn," said Fermin.

"Great!" said Gary. "This is all we need." He stood up and began to whistle for a wind. "Stick your knife into the mast, Blas," he said over his shoulder.

Blas obediently opened his clasp knife and thrust the tip of the blade into the mast. "That oughta do it," he said. "Had to kill a Hapon to get that knife. Made in Japan!"

"It will not work then," said Fermin.

The other Filipinos wisely nodded their heads in agreement.

An hour went by without any wind, but the night had grown much warmer. The cloud bank had moved closer. The swell was heavier, as though being driven by some force beneath the water.

Papa Alibongbong handed the tiller to Mama Rosalia and worked his way through the crowded interior of the boat to stand abaft the mast. He began to sing an odd-sounding, singsong sort of tune. Now and then he wet a finger and held it up, then shook his head. He began to whistle the same tune, blowing into the sail. Again he wet his finger and raised it. Bob did the same. He could have sworn the finger was cooler.

It was very quiet except for Papa Alibongbong whistling into the sail. Soon the sail flapped a little. The sweat dried on their faces. Papa Alibongbong kept on whistling into the flapping sail. A faint sound came over the swells. A swell slapped heavily against the side of the banca, showering the occupants with water. The sail flapped again and filled a little. Papa Alibongbong worked his way aft and took the tiller. The cloud bank was right over Verde Passage. The wind filled the sail, and the banca moved ahead. Suddenly the wind blew sharply, and the banca heeled hard over. Fermin and Abundio ran out on the tip-tilted outrigger arms. The banca settled down again. In a matter of minutes they were slashing through the swells. Whitecaps had begun to rise on the oily-looking water.

In an hour Bob was sorry Papa Alibongbong had whistled up a wind. The *bagools* scraped steadily, almost frantically, in the bottom of the banca. Icy rain slanted

156

down from the dark skies, soaking everyone to the skin. The equipment was protected by banigs well lashed down with abacá fiber, but there was no protection for the crew. Beyond the banca the night was a howling madness of waves, spray, rain, and wind. She plunged deeply and rose again, fighting to keep her head, with her sail filled hard with the roaring wind. Bob looked back at Papa Alibongbong. There was no fear on his thin face, and his clawlike hands did not shake on the tiller of hardwood as he steered his craft into the eye of the storm. Mama Rosalia too cast a proud eye at her beloved. There was no better banca skipper on Mindoro, but on the land, you understand, there was much to be desired in Papa Alibongbong.

Several hours passed, and the banca still sped on as though trying to drive herself under, but always miraculously, when it seemed she would surely dive, by some magic she rose shuddering to the seas and met the next swell with an easy motion.

Bob bailed steadily. "They oughta put pumps in these crazy boats," he said over his shoulder to Gary.

"Yeh!" said Gary. "*Yeh!*" he repeated.

"What's wrong?" yelled Bob.

"Look!" yelled Gary.

Bob looked over his shoulder. A high, V-shaped object was bearing down on them out of the pitchy darkness with a white froth of water at the bottom of it, curving back on both sides. He stared. "Destroyer!" he yelled at the top of his voice.

The banca swung a little. The sail flapped. Mama Alibongbong trimmed the sheet. The tin can was on them. It sped past doing a good twenty knots into the howling murk. Bob stared up at her salt-caked, rust-flecked sides. He could clearly see the great curving flare of the bows, the forward gun turrets and the bridge, with the sharply raked mast and even more sharply raked funnel typical of Japanese tin cans abaft the mast. The banca tilted far over, and water poured over her side. Blas and Fermin ran out on the outriggers. The great wash of the destroyer's wake foamed whitely into the rolling banca, and the tin can sped on into the night. Not a man had been seen on her rain-lashed decks, almost as though she did not have a crew.

They got the banca under control at last and bailed steadily for an hour to clear her. At last she finally sailed on with her usual gracefulness. The wind abated a little and then a lot until by four o'clock it was nothing but a fresh gale, dying steadily.

"Where do we hide?" yelled Blas at Fermin.

The pilot smiled. "No need to hide," he said. "The storm has blown us clear across the passage. The island we want is not far ahead, my friend."

Bob looked into the wet darkness. "How do you know, Fermin?" he asked.

The Filipino looked soberly at him. "I know," he said quietly. "Am I not a pilot?"

"Yeh," said Bob. He looked at Gary and shrugged. "He's a pilot, isn't he?"

Gary nodded. He emptied his *bagool*. "Yup, kiddo," he said. "You know it. I don't ask questions anymore after Papa Alibongbong whistled up that wind and that Hapon tin can missed us. It's a good thing they don't paint these crazy bancas. One coat of paint and that can would have hit us."

There was something to be seen faintly through the darkness. Papa Alibongbong stood up at the tiller. Fermin called soft directions to him. The darkness grew thicker, with a lighter line at the base of it. Palm trees could be made out. The banca was poked into a narrow inlet. The sail was furled and the mast unstepped and taken down.

"Over the side," said Papa Alibongbong. "Run her in, my friends!"

They splashed over the side into the dark water and worked the heavy log craft deep into the inlet. Undergrowth hung over the sides of the inlet and when they were far up it, the undergrowth closed in behind them like a leafy swinging door.

"Look," said Blas. He jerked a thumb upward.

The sky was starting to pale with the coming of the false dawn. A bird chirped in the darkness of the trees.

Bob picked up his carbine and slung it over his shoulder. He swung his belt about him and clasped it, settling it about his hips. He drew out the heavy Colt automatic and pulled back the slide to load it, putting on the safety catch before he returned the service pistol to its holster. "We'd better get out the gear and hide it," he said. "We don't know if there are Hapons on this island or not, and until we do, we'd better not take any chances."

The sun was up before they finished hiding the gear. Birds called and monkeys chattered in the trees. A warm wind blew across the island, and they could hear the dragging sound of the surf, which was still high after the night's storm.

"Who's in charge?" said Gary.

"Fermin," said Bob.

The Filipino raised his eyebrows. "I? I am only a pilot, not a military man."

"You've got to plot the minefields," said Blas.

"That I can do, but I am not a soldier," said the Filipino.

"Sailor!" growled Blas.

"Blas, you take charge," said Gary.

Blas shook his head. "I'm a seagoing sailor," he said. "You lads have had more experience in this kind of stuff than I have. One of you take over."

159

Gary looked at Bob. "Well?" he said.

"You're on," said Bob.

"I wasn't thinking of me, kiddo," said Gary. "It's you by unanimous consent."

"Well, thanks," said Bob dryly.

"What are your orders?" said Mama Rosalia.

Bob looked at his "powerful" command. Mild Fermin, and the boy Abundio, Mama and Papa Alibongbong, Blas and Gary. "Mama, you rustle up some chow. Blas, you go down to the mouth of the inlet and keep an eye out for Hapons either at sea or on the beaches. Abundio, take a pair of glasses and shinny up a tree to keep lookout. Gary and Fermin, come with me. Papa Alibongbong, you take charge of the camp here. Let's go! *Sigi legi, ho!*" He picked up a pair of the powerful glasses and walked into the thick growth of trees and vines.

Gary grinned as he trotted up beside Bob. "You put *Papa* in charge!"

Bob grinned back. "Listen!" he said.

The sound of angry voices speaking first in Tagalog came to them and then they distinctly heard Papa speak in English, "It is necessary to be quiet, woman! There may be Hapons about. *I* am in charge here and *I* say you must be quiet!" There was no further sound from Mama Rosalia. She knew better than to make too much noise. She'd bide her time. Papa would fall into her clutches sooner or later.

Bob and his two companions reached the beach area that faced the channel that had been mined by the Japanese. They lay down in the shelter of the coconut palms and Bob studied the channel with his glasses. There was nothing to be seen except the whitecapped waves still stirred up by the strong wind of the night before. "How do you plot a minefield, Fermin?"

The Filipino looked out toward the minefield. "It is

160

necessary to have the ship enter the minefield channel. We need distance, course, bearing, and speed taken every minute until the ship is out of sight." He withdrew a roll of paper from within his shirt and spread it out. "On here, one of us will mark the data. I will call out the data. Perhaps it will not take long if enough ships pass. There should be many of them. This is a busy channel, my friends."

Gary raised his head. "There's a small tanker now," he said.

"Let's make a dry run on this one," said Bob. "Just to get the feel of it. Gary, you record. I'll take a look-see up the beach. Far's I can see we have the island to ourselves, but you never know. If we get spotted on this island, our chances of escaping are about nil."

Bob watched Fermin and Gary as they prepared themselves. Fermin rested his glasses on a log of driftwood. "Time," he said. He had set the clock up beside him and had the compass with the pelorus arrangement. He put down the glasses and sighted through the compass. "Tanker! Distance 1800 yards! Time 0728 hours! Bearing 090! Course 275! Speed ten knots!" Gary wrote swiftly as Fermin called out the data. They acted like a team of experts.

Bob pushed his way through the tangle and reached a clearing through which a shallow stream wound its way to the sea. He waded to the far side and before he got out of the water he eyed the soft bank. There were no tracks other than those of animals. He walked along the length of a log that led into the tangle so as not to leave footprints.

Half a mile from the observation post he saw the burned-out hulk of a Type-A Daihatsu barge lying in the shallow water. A Japanese patrol plane droned toward Luzon. It was a big four-engined flying boat, one of the biggest Bob had ever seen. The tanker was still plowing through the channel with a creaming wake far behind her. Another craft was heaving into sight and heading for the channel. This time it was a *Chidori*-class patrol boat, fast and heavily armed. She was making a good fifteen knots. More meal for Fermin's mill.

A mile from the observation post he found *tabi* footprints in the soft earth beneath the trees, and recently made, for the heavy rains of days past would have washed out any others. In among the trees he found empty meat cans and paper candy wrappings left behind by the Japanese after they had eaten there. Evidently, as anticipated, they patrolled the uninhabited islands at intervals. Bob hoped with all his heart they would be able to get the plotting done and get off the island before a patrol came back. It wasn't likely. He saw a destroyer heaving into sight and heading for the minefield about a mile behind the *Chidori*-class patrol boat. It was a bustling place at that. The more ships the better, for that meant Fermin could get his job done all the faster.

He saw an ugly mine that had broken from its moorings in the minefield and had drifted ashore. He gave it a wide berth, eyeing its rusty shell and deadly horns with suspicion. The things were as touchy and as deadly as a rattlesnake. He had seen what they could do to a ship. His first ship in the Navy had been the *Craven*-class destroyer *MacRonan*, which had struck such a mine off Bougainville. Her whole bow and a large part of her forefoot and bottom had been blown clean off. She had gone down in a matter of minutes. He looked out at the minefield. It seemed so pleasant and peaceful out there, but if a ship blundered out of the channel through the mines, it would be blown up in a matter of seconds.

He saw several other mines lying on the beach and even as he watched he saw another bobbing in toward the shore, turning over lazily. The *Chibasco* of the night before had evidently broken a lot of them loose from their heavy moorings. The Japanese would know that such a storm would break mines loose and they would know too where the current set was, which meant they would know that some of the mines would drift ashore on this very island. "Great!" he said.

He walked back toward the observation post through the thick tangle, slashing long entangled vines with his bolo. He was getting good at it. He had had enough such experience in the past weeks ashore on Mindoro. The birds whistled and called, and the monkeys chattered in anger at this two-legged intruder. Something splashed in the shallow stream. Huge butterflies drifted past him on some aimless errand of their own. It was a lovely place, almost idyllic, for there seemed to be no mosquitoes, and wind off the sea was almost cool as it swept through the groves of coconut trees.

Fermin and Gary were too busy to take notice of Bob. The pilot was still calling off distance, course, bearing, and speed, which Gary swiftly took down in his neat hand-writing. They had already filled one sheet and were working on a second. Bob nodded his head in satisfaction. Granted that no Japanese patrols got too curious about the island, and that enough ships used the channel, it shouldn't take too long to finish the job. The sooner the better. The island was beautiful and peaceful, but there was an uneasy feeling gnawing away at Bob's mind.

Metal thudded against metal near the improvised camp of the little landing party. Bob bit his lip as he hurried toward the sound. There were no Japanese in sight off-shore, but if there were any lurking on the island, they were sure to hear that devil's chivaree echoing through the groves.

He heard Abundio yelling in Tagalog and Blas shouting incoherently in English. Bob flipped the safety off his carbine and trotted through the grove. They had been just too lucky so far. The metal clanged again and again. Bob burst into a shady clearing not far from the beach. Two figures crouched over a great, rusted rounded object. The metal clanged again as Papa Alibongbong smashed a length of auto spring leaf down on the rounded object. Bob's heart nearly failed. The little Filipino was pounding on a Japanese mine that had evidently been driven farther inshore than most of them, perhaps by the very typhoon that had nearly wrecked the guerrilla base camp on Mindoro.

Bob opened his mouth to yell, but the words would not come out of it, only a dry, spluttering sound. He saw Blas peering from behind a big, thick-boled coconut palm while Abundio hung in his lookout tree screaming down at his fellow guerrillas. Bob didn't know whether to hit the dirt or run and he couldn't do either. He seemed frozen in place. If that mine went off it would lay most of the grove flat and alert every Japanese within five miles, not that that made much difference, for there'd be no guerrillas left alive on the island anyway.

"Now, Papa!" screamed Mama Rosalia.

Papa Alibongbong smashed with his full strength. Bob didn't fall to the ground on purpose. His legs just gave way. Something clattered on the ground. Bob peered between his interlaced fingers. The mine access plate had dropped off leaving a neat hole into the interior. Mama Rosalia thrust in an eager hand. Bob was on his feet sprinting all out for cover. Blas had vanished into the stream, wallowing and splashing across like an amtrac.

Abundio also had vanished, although Bob had no idea whether he had fallen from the tree or not.

Bob hit the dirt and slid for home, rolling over a huge palm log and clawing industriously at the soft earth with his naked hands while cold sweat dropped from his face. He was down a full foot when he heard the curious voice behind him.

"You got a wrench, kiddo? What you doing?"

He looked up into the calm face of Mama Rosalia.

"You—you—" It was no use. Bob's voice died away and he placed his face against the ground.

"You got a wrench or not, kiddo?" persisted the woman.

Bob looked up at her. "Why do you want a wrench?" he asked in a soft little voice.

"Got to take the guts out of that mine, kiddo."

"Why?" pleaded Bob.

She stared at him. "Powder, man! Enough powder to blow up this whole island. Man, we're rich! Papa Alibong-bong can get all the fish he wants now."

"With the mine?" asked Bob patiently.

She shook her head. "You take out the powder and mix it with water. Then you let it dry into blocks. You wrap the blocks in a lot of layers of rattan weighted with stones. Papa hunts for fish under coral. Lowers powder and touches it off. Whoooooeeee! More crazy fish than you ever saw in your whole life, kiddo!"

Bob sat up and wiped the dirt from his face. He reached into his pocket and withdrew a wrench. "That all right?" he asked.

"Peachy keen, kiddo," she said.

"May I ask why you want a wrench after you have *hammered* the access plate off?"

"Got to take out the mechanical guts, kiddo. Papa Alibongbong has a hobby. You know. Spare parts. Crazy mine is full of them. Toodle-oo, Mac." She waddled off toward her spouse and the mine.

Bob poked his head above the log. Papa Alibongbong had one arm inside the mine up to the shoulder and was feeling around with an intent look on his face. Bob went down behind the log again. "More crazy fish than you ever saw in your whole life, kiddo!" He shook his head. "Whooooeeee!"

16 ...

Bob slapped his hand against his thigh in disgust. "It's no use!" he snapped. "This radio is out! Completely out! Of all the rotten luck!"

"We can take the data back by the banca," said Blas.

"No!" said Bob. "We can't take a chance. We've been here three days, and every day we see more patrol boats and planes. You saw them stop two bancas yesterday not half a mile offshore. You heard that machine gun fire. You know what was left of that second banca when the patrol boat left. Swamped and sinking with four dead Filipinos in it. It isn't *our* lives I'm thinking of. I'm thinking of our ships coming into this passage with inadequate information or none at all. We haven't got the time to fool around, Blas!"

"Take it easy, kid," said Blas. He rubbed the stubble on his chin. "Beats me. Brand-new 88 and not a peep out of it."

"I've checked every tube, lead, and even the screws that hold the crazy box together, and I get nothing. Absolutely nothing!"

Blas glanced sideways at Bob. "Take it easy," he warned. "You're acting as if you were island happy."

Bob leaned back against a tree and closed his eyes.

167

"Maybe I am, Blas. It's too much. Every night I think I hear patrol boats offshore. Last night I could have sworn I heard Jap voices in the wind."

Gary came through the grove. "Fermin says we've got all the data we need," he said.

"It's useless," said Abundio.

"We could make copies and take them separately," said Papa Alibongbong.

"In *one* banca?" said Gary scornfully.

Bob shook his head. "We'll have to risk taking them in the banca tonight," he said. He looked up at the others. "If we're caught, you know what will happen to us."

There was no answer. From high overhead came the droning of an enemy patrol plane. There were twice as many over the passage as there had been less than a week ago. The Hapons were suspicious. They smelled trouble on the tropical wind.

The engine thudded away, echoing through the grove. Every time Blas kicked the engine over, Bob's heart flopped. Every time he did so he could have sworn it got louder and louder and *louder!* Maybe he was a little "island happy." It came eventually to all servicemen who had spent too much time in combat zones, even the bravest of them. He had seen men go blind whose sight was perfect. He had seen a Marine go berserk and wound two of his best friends before he had been subdued. Another had received the Navy Cross and that night had walked into the jungle and shot himself. Twice men had disappeared from the *Logie*, and no one had ever known whether they had fallen overboard or had taken what seemed to be the easy way out. It was the plodders like Blas who managed to keep going on and on and on.

Gary idly flipped his sheath knife over and over in his hand and let it drop point first into the soft earth. "Something Mr. Kelly said," he said softly.

"Like what?" asked Blas.

Gary shook his head. He narrowed his eyes. He looked at the dirt around them. "*Something* he said. I can't remember."

Mama Rosalia poked her head from behind a stunted tree. "Patrol boat cruising half a mile offshore," she said. "Looking this way with glasses. Can see sun sparkle on them. Half a mile good range for a bazooka, kiddos?"

"Git!" snapped Blas.

"No way to talk to a lady," she grumbled as she vanished.

Gary looked about. They had moved their camp farther along the shore to where a low bluff thrust itself into the sea. There were caves within the bluff where they could hide if necessary. It was about the only place on the island where they *could* hide. "You notice how red this earth is compared to Mindoro?" he said thoughtfully. "Look at the crazy trees. They're only about half the size they should be, and all twisted out of shape."

"What of it?" said Blas.

Gary stabbed his knife deeply into the reddish earth. "This crazy island is like a big block of iron, that's *what!* We've got too much interference, at least for that 88."

"Out of the mouths of babes and sucklings," said Blas.

"What's a suckling?" said Gary. "I thought that was a pig."

"You guessed it, kid," said Blas.

Bob stood up. Gary was right. Perhaps back at the original camp in the coconut grove was a better spot, but it was too open and exposed, and besides it was three miles up the beach. By the time they got the gear down there and set up again it would mean the loss of a day, and even then, they couldn't be sure the radio would work any better.

"What's the answer?" said Blas.

169

Bob picked up a pair of glasses. "Wait," he said. He scrambled up the slope and took cover at the top of the bluff. He could see the patrol boat moving offshore, with bare steerageway on it. The sun glinted from something on the bridge. They were thoroughly scanning the shore with the excellent Japanese glasses. Those glasses had been another of the surprises the supposedly inadequate Japanese Navy had come up with, like the Zeros that had made monkeys out of the earlier American pursuit ships. Bob studied the shore. The bluff hooked in a little, leaving a semi-exposed cove that faced toward Mindoro. He nodded and scrambled down the hill.

"Well?" said Gary.

"We can anchor the banca offshore in that cove and set the radio up in it to avoid interference," said Bob.

"Out *there?*" said Blas. "You *are* island happy!"

"Look," said Bob fiercely. "We can't stay here much longer! Fermin told us the Hapons patrol these islands about once a week on the average, so they're due here any day! Maybe even today! We've got the information, and they need it desperately back at Headquarters. If we can get it to Mindoro this afternoon, it will be in Australia this evening! We don't know when The Aid *is* due, but from the looks of things back on Mindoro, it must be very soon!"

Blas shoved back his battered straw hat. "You win, kid. I'll do the transmitting."

"Too slow, Blas."

They all looked at Bob. Silently they began to gather together what gear he would need. They carried it to the shore of the cove where the banca was hidden in a narrow inlet. Bob set up the gear in the boat and covered it with several banigs placed on top of paddles run thwartwise across the log hull of the boat. He was scared to go but he knew he'd be a lot more scared sitting on the island or out in the passage with a patrol boat bearing down on

170

them. He remembered all too well seeing a patrol boat overhaul a banca offshore and the faint stuttering of a Nambu, and then the sight of the wallowing banca left behind by the patrol boat. They had taken no prisoners.

No one spoke. There was nothing to say. Anything would be superfluous. None of the others could do anything except watch. Papa Alibongbong and Abundia hoisted the mast with the aerial attached to it. Bob got into the banca and placed his carbine in the bottom of it. He took Gary's thoroughly bedraggled straw hat with the faded red-wool balls hanging around the brim and clapped it on his bare head. They shoved him off, and he paddled the heavy craft out into the open water. Seventy feet from the shore he was free of the lee of the bluff, which would interfere with his sending, blocking him off from Mindoro. He could see clear across the choppy waters of the passage. The patrol boat had moved on toward the other end of the island. He hoped they didn't have detecting gear aboard. They might get a fix from another boat or a shore station and pin him down as he transmitted. If they did, none of the guerrillas would ever leave that island alive. He knew they knew that. None of them had mentioned it, but they knew the incredibly dangerous game they were playing. They knew it all too well.

He anchored the banca and grounded the wire in the water. He checked the batteries and the leads. It took all the nerve he had to put on the earphones and open contact with FFTP on Mindoro. He was answered right away. He started to transmit. The wind was shifting and variable. It was almost the end of August. Sometimes the wind blew strongly from the northeast and then from the southwest, and as he transmitted the first sheet of data the wind came from both directions at the same time with increased force. The passage began to work up into a froth. Wash surged into the cove, wallowing the heavy banca, and crashed on the shore, withdrawing with a rattling, dragging sound. The wind moaned through the bending trees. Spray dashed up from the sides of the banca almost as if she were underway. Bob was soon soaked to the skin and the data paper was damp, but he managed to keep the radio dry.

Something rolled beneath him, and he reached under and picked up one of the pieces of Shelby tubing that Mama Rosalia had tossed to him the night they had left Mindoro. He angrily hurled it full force into the stern of the boat. She was like a scavenger or a thieving magpie. Anything was grist for the mill to Mama Rosalia.

The water got choppier and choppier, heaving the boat back and forth. The radio thudded against the side of the banca, and he was forced to stop transmitting to pad the side of the radio. A couple more wallops like that and the 88 would be out of business. He finished the second sheet and reached for the third. The spray was already dimming Gary's neat handwriting, and it was hard to read the figures. They had to be absolutely accurate or they were no good at all.

Bob lay down in the bottom of the boat trying to protect the data paper from the increasing spray. He finished the third sheet and picked up the fourth. An odd swishing sound came to him. He raised his head and looked over the side of the boat. Couldn't be the waves. He looked up, and his blood seemed to congeal into icy red crystals. Directly overhead, not one hundred and fifty feet above the cove, was a Japanese float plane. The slide at the rear part of the greenhouse had been pushed back, and a helmeted head was thrust through the opening with a pair of glasses held to the eyes, *and he was looking directly down at Bob!*

Bob ripped off the telltale earphones. He reached over

and jerked the aerial free from the mast. It fell atop him and he pushed it aside. The plane swung downwind, banked, and the engine roared into noisy life. The plane climbed and then turned again. The engine cut out and the pilot began his glide directly toward Bob and the island. There was no landing strip on the island, and anyway it was a float plane. The thought ran through Bob's thoroughly frightened mind that there was nothing he could do. *Absolutely nothing!*

Cold sweat poured down his sides, and his mouth and throat went brassy dry. His heart leaped erratically. The plane was directly overhead, but he did not look up at it, half expecting to hear a bomb drop into the water beside him or hear the stuttering of machine guns. The plane flew beyond him. The engine roared, spitting back exhaust smoke, and the plane flew out toward sea, banked again, with the sun flashing on the greenhouse, and then flew toward Luzon.

"Get going!" yelled Blas from the shore. "Don't take any more chances, kid. You've done your share!"

Maybe he won't come back, thought Bob. He prayed a little. He lowered the mast and attached the aerial to it. He had a hard time getting the mast up in the teeth of the strong and shifting wind. It slid into the step, and he dropped beside the radio, sick and faint with weakness and fear. He opened contact again. It took a full hour to finish. He grinned weakly as he signed off. Shadows hung across the cove. The sun was low down.

"Bob!" yelled Blas. "Come on in!"

He nodded. "In a couple of minutes!" he called back.

"*Now!*" yelled Blas. "Look offshore!"

Bob looked over his shoulder. Fear struck at him again. A patrol boat was heading directly toward the cove, at least a mile offshore, spurting up a white spray of bow

173

wave. Bob grabbed a paddle and started toward shore. Halfway to shore he met Blas and Gary, who were swimming out to him. They swam on either side of the banca, driving it in toward the beach. The others met them in armpit-deep water, and they all forced the banca into the inlet and stripped it of the radio gear. Mama Rosalia grabbed up her two bits of Shelby tubing and stored them in her more than ample bosom. They struggled through the tangle behind the beach, carrying or dragging the gear. Bob was reminded of an illustration he had once seen, drawn by N. C. Wyeth, in which a group of pirates were hauling a treasure chest onto some unnamed Caribbean island.

Abundio dropped behind to watch the oncoming boat. The rest of them hauled the gear into a cave and then cut growths to cover the mouth of it. "What do we do?" said Gary. "Scatter?"

Blas shook his head. "If they land, they'll get us all if we scatter." He unslung his carbine. "We fight," he said. "They're not going to take Mrs. Blascovitz' favorite son Stanislaus alive."

The big cook was right. If they scattered and ran, the Hapons would hunt them down like rabbits and kill them anyway. At that, to fight was a desperate measure, for those patrol boats carried big crews as well as strong landing parties.

"She's coming on fast!" yelled Abundio.

Mama Rosalia picked up her bazooka. "Eight rounds," she said. "I wish I had my own cannon, kiddos."

Papa Alibongbong looked admiringly at her. "One shot is enough for you, my beloved."

She nodded. "That is so, my little chicken."

"Do not let them take me alive," said Papa.

She shook her head. "Nor me, Papa."

174

He swallowed hard. "I cannot do that, my pigeon."

"You will, Papa," she said, "you will when the time comes."

The two of them vanished into the brush.

"Can you beat that?" said Blas in astonishment.

Bob couldn't help laughing, no matter how frightened he was. "One of the great love stories of all time, Jerry Hoffman said. Romeo and Juliet. Hero and Leander. Lord Horatio Nelson and Lady Hamilton."

They pushed their way through the tangle. Mama had crawled up the slope and placed her bazooka between two rocks. She settled her shoulder against the weapon. Papa loaded it and tapped her shoulder. She nodded.

The patrol boat was two hundred yards off the mouth of the cove. It turned a little. Mama tightened her hand on the grip and pressed the slack out of the trigger.

Closer and closer it came until it was in perfect range for a shot. Mama drew in a deep breath.

"Wait!" shouted Fermin. "It's one of ours! A PT boat! I know them well! It is perhaps The Aid!"

"The Aid!" shrieked Abundio. He leaped from cover and danced about waving his arms at the oncoming boat.

Bob felt an icy stab of fear. "Wait!" he snapped. He grabbed a pair of glasses.

"It is The Aid! The Aid!" yelled Abundio as he danced about in full view.

The glasses were focused on the PT boat. It was a sure-enough PT all right, thought Bob. He focused on the bow gunner and then on the man at the controls and his heart nearly stopped. "Hapons!" he yelled. "That's a captured boat!"

"Get down, you crazy fool!" shouted Blas at Abundio.

Gary neatly tackled the excited Filipino boy. It was too late. The PT swung sideways. "Shoot!" screamed Bob.

The bazooka jerked and cracked, shooting flame and smoke. The projectile struck the side of the boat. Bob saw the splinters fly, but there was no explosion. "Shoot! Shoot!" he barked.

Papa Alibongbong reloaded the bazooka and slapped Mama on the shoulder. Once again she fired. Once again splinters flew from the side of the boat, but there was no inner explosion.

Bob dropped the glasses and looked at the remaining six rounds of bazooka ammunition and his heart sank. It was delayed-action shell used on tanks. It was going right through both sides of the wooden hull and splashing harmlessly into the sea on the other side of the PT boat. Mama fired twice more and missed. Her next shot tore splinters from the deck. A gun opened fire from the afterdeck, and tracers skipped across the water and then raised. A hail of slugs whipped through the trees and brush. Everyone hit the dirt except Mama Rosalia. She fired and missed. Her seventh shot hit the after gun and tore it off its mountings. It tumbled overside into the sea, dragging the hapless gunner with it. She fired her last round. It struck the sea and ricocheted over the speeding boat. Rifles and machine guns opened up from the boat, and Japanese after Japanese came up on deck carrying bayoneted rifles. The sun struck shards of light from the naked, razor-edged blades. There were at least thirty on the deck by the time the boat was reaching the shallows.

"Imperial Marines!" said Gary. "We've had it!"

Abundio fired his carbine.

"Wait!" said Bob. "Don't waste ammunition! Let them get closer.

Mama Rosalia cast aside her bazooka. "Come on, Papa!" she yelled. She ran clumsily out on the miniature headland that overlooked the cove, thrusting a hand inside her dress. She withdrew it. The sun shone warmly on a piece of the Shelby tubing she held. Papa Alibongbong was trotting after his big wife, calmly lighting a twisted, horrible-smelling Filipino cigar.

Blas shook his head. "He's either the calmest man I ever saw in my life or he's lost his marbles. Lookit him smoking at a time like this!"

Bob narrowed his eyes. He raised his carbine. The Marines were going over the side, landing waist-deep in the clear water, some of them wading ashore in a bunch. "Banzai! Banzai! Banzai!" they shrieked. One of them had a Rising Sun flag attached to his bayonet. An officer waved a glittering samurai blade.

Mama casually held back her hand, holding the piece of tubing, and Papa held the lighted end of the cigar to the piece of string or cord that hung down from the tubing. "Now, Mama!" he said.

She held the tubing and its spluttering fuze, slowly counting to herself. She hurled it down toward the charging Marines and then dropped as light machine-gun fire raked the ground just in front of her. The tubing splashed into the water right in among the Marines and exploded. A towering spout of water blossomed whitely and here and there strange objects flew through the air. The smoke and spray drifted off, and where the Marines had been was a widening circle of water but there were no Marines, or at least none on their feet.

Mama held back the second piece of tubing. Papa lighted the fuze. Mama counted and threw the tubing with a long overarm swing so that it arced upward and dropped, turning end over end to drop on top of the foredeck of the boat. It exploded as it struck. Sailors, Marines, and pieces of plywood were hurled up and outward. The boat shuddered and ran aground, tilting to one side.

177

Smoke arose from the shattered foredeck. Japanese dropped shrieking over the side into the roiled water.

There was no command necessary on the little headland. Carbines and rifles flashed and crashed. The panicked Japanese either went down or plunged into the brush, completely demoralized. In three minutes there wasn't a living Japanese to be seen in or near the smoking boat. A runnel of flame licked along the shattered remnants of the foredeck.

Blas stood up and reloaded his carbine. "If we want that plywood soap dish," he said, "we'd better go down and put out that fire. Fire-control party, yo!" He plunged down the hill, missed his footing, and went crashing into the trees at the bottom of the grade.

The rest of them reloaded and followed the big cook. Cautiously they waded out to the boat. There was no sign of life. Lifeless Marines bobbed in the rolling surf. Bob and Blas gave Gary and Abundio a hand up onto the deck to put out the fire. Gary whistled sharply. "What a crazy mess!" he said. "Come on, fellows! There's no one here. At least no one here *alive*."

Bob clambered up on the deck from Blas's shoulders. He threw down a rope's end for the others. He stared in astonishment at what had been the foredeck. "What was in that tubing, Mama Rosalia?" he asked.

She smiled. "I invented it, kiddo. Eight inches of Shelby tubing, grooved with a file so it would bust into pieces. Three sticks of dynamite worked into it. Two-inch fuse. Man, it sure busted 'em wide open, hey, kiddo?"

Bob nodded. He went a little pale, and his stomach heaved a little. He remembered all too well when Mama Rosalia had carelessly tossed those two lethal pieces of tubing to him the night they were getting ready to leave Mindoro. He remembered them rolling around in the bilge of the banca throughout the storm, sometimes trodden upon by the crew. Worst of all he remembered feeling one of them beneath him as he worked the 88 in the banca offshore and how he had angrily hurled it with full force into the stern of the banca. *"Oi vey,"* he said weakly.

The sun was almost gone. Thick shadows felt their way out into the cove. Inside the PT a Packard motor kicked over and idled gently. Blas thrust his head up out of a hatch. "We got one engine anyway," he said.

"You aim to take this wreck back to Mindoro?" said Gary incredulously.

"Why not?" said Blas. "We can make better time than that banca, and we could use a *real* fighting craft in the Coconut Patrol."

"He's got a point there," said Gary. He looked at Bob.

Bob rubbed his jaw. He was tired and could hardly think. The thought of sailing back through those dark waters with the banca wasn't very appealing. At least they'd have a fighting chance with the PT boat, battered and holed as she was. "O.K.," he said at last. "Plug all the holes. Get the pumps started. We've got to get her afloat."

It was fully dark when they started two of the engines. All of them except Blas ran aft and then back and forth across the deck, rocking the lean hull until at last she broke the bottom suction and drifted into deeper water. There was a short wait while Papa Alibongbong got his banca from the inlet. They fastened its painter to the stern of the PT boat.

"What about the radio?" said Gary.

"I wouldn't go back on that island for anything," said Bob.

"You said it, kiddo," said Gary.

Bob took the controls. As he steered toward the open sea, he could feel intense vibration pounding through the

179

hull. Bent propeller shaft probably, or perhaps a blade had been twisted or broken off. Still, it was better than a banca. The Filipinos and Gary placed banigs across the gaping hole in the foredeck and lashed them taut to keep out the spray that was dashing over the flared bows as the PT met the scend of the open water. It promised to be a rough passage.

Blas turned over the engine room to Fermin and then rummaged in the galley. In the thick darkness before the rising of the moon he served the improvised meal. "Not bad, fellows," he said. "These boys ate good. We got *amanatto*—that's sugared red beans. Sweet bean jelly— that's *yokan*—and *daifuki mochi*. That's rice cakes stuffed with bean paste. There's some dried squid too. I don't remember the name of that."

"Forget it," said Gary.

By the time the moon had crept up, the thickly wooded shores of Mindoro were in sight.

17...

THEY SET UP a grid when the tide had flowed out of the mangrove swamp, placing heavy timbers where the bottom of the damaged PT boat would rest and spiking them firmly together. When the tide came back in, the PT boat was hauled over the grid by means of a hawser wound around an improvised windlass barrel set up on the shore. It took some straining and sweating, but at last the eighty-foot Elco PT boat was in the right position. She was moored so that she would not drift from her position. All the guerrillas had to do was to wait until the tide went out.

Colonel Bledsoe had imported Pop MacLean, veteran of the old Navy, who had taken his discharge in the Philippines after the insurrection to start his own boatyard on Mindoro. The aged Scot showed up late one night in a battered Japanese truck loaded with tools and odds and ends, and with his working crew of half a dozen Filipinos. While Pop inspected the musty, cockroach-ridden inside of the hull, the guerrillas and Mangyans swarmed up into the mangroves and strung vines and ropes of abacá fiber across the area above the boat. In three hours they had woven a concealing mat of plaited leaves to conceal the PT from prying Japanese aerial eyes. In addition they hung a plaited mat on a roller that could be pulled down behind the boat like a window shade to conceal it from a seaward view, although it was already pretty well concealed by the tangled vegetation between the swamp proper and the beach.

Pop shouted his orders to his crew in a weird mixture of Scots dialect, proper English, Americanese, Tagalog, and Spanish, touching it up now and then with a few expressive words in various dialects. As they say in Scotland: "Yon Pop MacLean is a man o' pairts!"

Bob, Gary, and Blas gave Pop a hand. Bob and Gary had served aboard a PT boat in the Solomons, and Blas, like most old-time sailors, was a handyman who could do just about anything reasonably well in the matter of ships and boats. The Elco had three twelve-cylinder Packard engines that could bring the boat up to a speed of close to fifty knots, or nearly fifty-seven land miles an hour, with a full load, but she had been in service too long, both in American and Japanese hands, and had seen far better days. Still, there was plenty of power left in the engines. The hull had taken a terrible beating. Although called plywood boats, they were really built of two layers of mahogany planking laid over laminated wood frames with a layer of airplane fabric glued between the two layers of planking. It resulted in a lightweight hull that was resilient and sturdy enough to stand up in heavy seas. Plywood was used only in the deck and superstructure. A few precious sheets had been brought down by Pop, and his boys set to work replacing the shattered foredeck while others whittled hardwood plugs and drove them into the many bullet holes. The larger holes were covered with either sheet metal or plywood. Fractured frames were braced on either side and bolted through. Pop was a great believer in the use of wire and rawhide in such matters. Wet rawhide was wrapped as tightly as possible around some of the frames and allowed to dry, drawing up like a vise.

Blas inspected the four torpedo tubes. Two of them were empty and two were loaded. "I wonder how long these tin fish have been in here," he mused.

"Probably since Bataan," said Bob.

"I can check the firing mechanism. I can't guarantee these things will work or even leave the tubes."

"We do the best we can," said Gary. He looked dubiously at the greased noses of the torpedoes. "I think we ought to get rid of 'em."

"Yeh," said Blas, "but what if we could get a crack at a Jap cruiser or maybe even one of those goofy-looking carriers they got! Man!"

" 'Man' is right," said Bob dryly. "How close do you think you'd get? Every one of their carriers has gobs of destroyers around it and heavy air coverage."

"Well, a fellow can dream, can't he?"

"More like a nightmare," said Gary.

The turrets abaft the cockpit still had the original twin fifty-caliber machine guns in each of them. Gary checked them out. There was plenty of captured ammunition for them. The fore and aft guns, whatever they had been, most likely Japanese guns, had both been lost when the guerrillas had attacked the craft. Both of them had been blown overboard, along with the gunners. On boats in the U.S. Navy these would be 20mm. guns, but there wasn't a one to be had on Mindoro. Mama Rosalia's famous cannon was absolutely banned by Gary. When Mama Rosalia saw the young sailor working on the four fifty-caliber guns, she knew she had been betrayed, for there had been a real gunner serving with her *boroba* after all. The glint in her dark eyes boded no good for Gary Lunt, Gunner's Mate Third Class, once he was free from his duties on the PT boat.

The main problem was the propulsion of the boat. Two of the propeller shafts and shaft housings had been bent.

It was that which had caused the throbbing vibration in the boat during her journey across Verde Passage to Mindoro. Bob shook his head as he saw them. It was a job that could only be handled by a well-equipped boatyard.

Pop MacLean stood knee-deep in the stinking mud eyeing the shafts. "Aye," he said thoughtfully, "they maun be in awfu' shape, lad, I'll nae deny it."

"We can run her on the one prop," said Bob. "But we'd be bested by a garbage scow if we tried to outrun a Jap patrol boat or tin can."

"Aye," said the old Scot. He rubbed his gingery whiskers. The moonlight filtered through the leaves. "There's a way." He looked back over his shoulder. "Cinco!" he yelled. "On the double here!"

A muscular, squat Filipino splashed through the mud. Pop explained the situation to him in his weird conglomeration of languages, and what was more weird was that Cinco understood him. They pulled the propellers and shafts from the bent shaft housings and hauled them to dryer land. Men set to work immediately to straighten them out.

Bob watched Pop and Cinco as they worked on the first bent housing. They centered a wire through it and placed a light at the inboard end of the housing. Pop squinted down the tube. "Bang away, me lad," he said.

Cinco braced himself on the grid and swung a ten-pound hammer with powerful ease against the shaft housing. It rang like a cracked bell. Bob shook his head. "Wasting your time," he said.

There was no answer. Again and again the hammer thudded against the shaft housing while Pop eyed the wire, gauging it against the inner sides of the polished shaft housing. "Enough, Cinco!" he cried. "Now the ither one, me friend."

184

Bob looked down the straightened shaft housing. It seemed true to him, but he couldn't be sure. An hour went by while Pop and Cinco worked on the second shaft housing, which was rather badly bent. It had been in such poor shape that Bob had not used that engine for fear the vibration would lift the heavy Packard from its bedding.

Meanwhile, on the shore they had heated the shafts, and under the direction of a wizened old Filipino blacksmith, who looked at least eighty years old and more fitted to the deck of a Malay pirate prau than a modern PT boat, the shafts were straightened. Other Filipinos filed the edges of the nicked propeller blades.

It took a week of hard, unremitting labor to get the PT in reasonable enough shape to take to the water again. High octane gas had been scrounged from every possible place on the island to fill the three fuel tanks, each of which required a thousand gallons. Much of it had been siphoned from a Japanese light bomber that had crashed without flaming into the treetops, which had cushioned its fall. The tanks had been almost full. When the tanks of the PT had been filled, there wasn't an eyedropperful of high-octane gas anywhere on Mindoro. A Japanese Nambu heavy machine gun had been located to mount on the forward deck and a rusty 37mm. antitank gun for the afterdeck, relic of the equipment used by the American forces when the Japanese had invaded the Philippines. The barrel was badly worn, but there was antitank and contact explosive shells for it in a good quantity.

"She's a' done," said Pop MacLean late one afternoon as he wiped the sweat from his bald head. "There's nae mair can be done wi' her, the poor lassie. We've done oor best, we have. The rest is up tae ye lads. Guid luck tae ye' a', laddies." He was gone as swiftly as he had appeared,

185

driving his battered, listing Japanese truck into the shadows.

Gary squatted on a slimy mangrove root, moodily eyeing the rejuvenated boat. He looked like an unhappy, bedraggled crow. "Guid luck tae ye a', laddies," he mimicked. "Now that we've got her done, what do we do with her?"

"She needs a crew," said Blas. He patted the patched side. "I've had enough of land warfare, mates. It's me for the sea."

"It's you for a large hole in the head," said Gary scornfully.

"You too chicken to take a ride in this baby?" said Blas. He held out his hand to Eugene, who happily scampered down from the deck of the boat. "Eugene isn't."

"Eugene is as loco in the head as you are," said Gary. "I didn't say I wouldn't go as crew, but I'd still like to know what is going to be done with her. We can't fight the patrol boats the Japs got out there. Too many of them, and most of them are better armed than we are. We run into a *Chidori*-class patrol boat and we run right outa this world, Mac. They could whop shells through us like a needle going through cloth."

"We're not aiming to fight them," said Blas stubbornly.

"Well, Mac, whether you know it or not, *they're* aiming to fight *you*."

Bob looked back through the swamp to the dimly lighted shack where Colonel Bledsoe had set up his temporary headquarters. By shortwave radio he communicated with the broadcast radio station FFTP, which was being operated in the hills, relaying intelligence matter to Darwin and GHQ-SWPA. They had fed a lot of material to headquarters. The plotted minefield channels, numbers, tonnage and types of enemy ships passing through Verde Passage, numbers and calibers of enemy gun installations on Luzon and other islands, numbers of troops, air traffic and activities, directions, numbers and types of planes, possible air routes, constant weather reports, as well as data on every possible enemy installation for potential targets, particularly in and around Manila Bay and in Verde Passage. Top-secret written and memorized reports had poured in and had been sent out. Men had died swiftly or slowly and horribly if they had been caught by the Japanese while carrying some of this information.

"What month is this?" asked Gary as he inspected an insect bite on his arm.

"August," said Blas.

"September," said Bob.

"So I lost a week or two," said Blas.

"When is The Aid due?" said Abundio from the deck of the PT boat.

"¿Quien sabe?" said Gary. "I been wondering if it will ever come."

Bob shrugged. Maps and other information had been sent out by American submarines in the past weeks for the use of the invading forces, when and if they'd ever come. Bob had just about given up hope.

Colonel Bledsoe came through the shadows and looked up at the repaired boat. "Ready for sea?" he said quietly.

"Yes, sir," said Bob.

Bledsoe looked at Bob. "Can you handle her, son?"

"I've handled them, sir," said Bob, "both in the Aleutians and in the Solomons."

"Steering?"

Bob looked quickly at the officer. "Yes, sir."

"What I want to know is whether you can handle her. *Command* her, is the better word. In combat, that is, son."

It was very quiet in the swamp except for the faint sighing of the wind through leaves and the rumbling sound of the surf. A Filipino laughed in the distance. Gary Lunt cleared his throat.

"Well?" said the officer.

"I'm only a Signalman Second Class, sir."

"I haven't yet seen you botch a job, Bob. We need this boat in a hurry. I haven't anyone else who has had the experience you've had on this type of craft. Would you rather I ask Blas or Gary?"

Blas shook his head. "He'll need me on the engines, sir."

"I'm the gunner," said Gary.

"Fermin can pilot you," said the colonel.

Bob remembered all too well sailing across Verde Passage in the banca, feeling like a chip in the bathtub when that Japanese tin can had come down on them out of nowhere. He remembered all too well limping back across Verde Passage in the badly battered PT boat, expecting a Japanese patrol boat or submarine to nail them any second, or perhaps a Japanese patrol plane to find them. He was scared.

"I can't go," said the officer. "I'm needed here now more than I ever was."

"Jap attack due, sir?" asked Blas.

The colonel shook his head. "It's The *Aid*, lads. The Third Fleet is already launching carrier-based plane attacks on Manila Bay and other Luzon targets." That was as far as he got. Blas and Bob grabbed Gary from his roost on the mangrove root and threw him headfirst into a stinking tidal pool. Gary came up spluttering and hit Blas with a rotted fish. Fermin heaved a can full of grease and oil over Bob's head. Bob retaliated with a gob of foul mud. In two minutes the fight had spread among the Filipinos all through the area around the PT boat. In the thick of the action Bob scooped up a shovelful of mud and aimed it at Blas. Blas dived to one side, and the mud hit

188

Colonel Bledsoe full in his official face. He went down on top of Gary, who once again went back into his tidal pool.

It was very quiet as Bledsoe struggled out of the hole and sat down in the foul mud, wiping it from his eyes and mouth. For one awful moment he stared at Bob with his one uncovered eye. "You never did answer me," he said reproachfully.

"After all that, what else can I do but volunteer?" said Bob. "Life will never be the same in the old *boroba* after this."

They helped the colonel to his feet and wiped him off as best they could. "One of our jobs is to fish downed aviators out of Verde Passage and the South China Sea," he said. "I plan to use every Coconut Patrol banca, baroto and *caba-caba* we've got."

"And we go along, sir?" said Blas.

The officer shook his head. "There's something else that has to be done. Something we have to do before our surface craft come into Verde Passage." He hesitated for a moment. "You've heard of the Q-boats?"

Bob felt sick inside. The very name gave him an uneasy feeling. "Yes, sir," he said quietly.

"We've found out what they are, and what's more we know where some of them are concentrated. Before our surface craft risk Verde Passage we'll have to do something about them and the only craft we have available to do it is this PT boat."

"What are they?" asked Gary in a strained voice.

"Small boats made of light wood about thirteen or fourteen feet long, with hardwood bows, powered by converted automobile engines, steered by a wheel in the center of the boat. Decked most of their length, painted a dull olive-green. Carry a two-man crew."

Gary grinned. "Well, well," he said. "We oughta have a

field day with them! Thirteen or fourteen feet long you say, sir. Well, well!"

Bob was watching the colonel's muddy face. He wasn't smiling. Bledsoe lighted a cigar and blew a smoke ring through which he poked a strong finger. "They are loaded chock-full of explosives, sonny," he said quietly. "The idea is for them to sneak up on our surface craft. They can hardly be seen against the background of the shoreline. They go only *one* way—to the surface craft. They plan to ram with them. In short, suicide missions."

Once again it was very quiet. The uneasy guerrillas looked at each other. One thought was in all their minds. If Q-boats could ram larger ships, they'd have a field day with the PT boat. If the PT gunners hit them at close range, they could blow up and take the PT right along with them. *Suicide mission . . .* It worked both ways.

"Fermin knows that coast," said Bledsoe. "There are large concentrations of Q-boats in Balayan Bay and Batangas Bay that have to be wiped out. Our Navy plans to send in PT boats, but they are not here as yet. The surface craft can't wait too long. So it's up to you, lads."

"When do we leave, sir?" said Blas.

"As soon as I get the word. One advantage you'll most likely have is that the Japs might recognize your boat and think it is still manned by their men. I'll check up and see when you should leave." He waded through the mud and walked to the radio shack.

"Some advantage," said Abundio.

Gary nodded. "He said *'most likely.'* "

Bob climbed the rickety wooden ladder to the deck. "Let's get her ready for sea," he said quietly.

But the word didn't come for many days. The PT boat, by now named *Bahála Ná,* or *Come What May,* had other work cut out for it. They picked up downed United States

Navy aviators at sea and on small islands, although twice they found aviators lying dead, their arms bound behind them and countless bayonet thrusts through their bodies. They ferried raiding parties of guerrillas and picked up intelligence officers from GHQ-SWPA who were brought in by submarine. They learned also that *Grayfin* was attached to the Third Fleet, somewhere in the South China Sea. September slipped past and October, and then November arrived, and with it the news that United States surface craft were due in Verde Passage. This time they received all the gasoline they required with little trouble, carried in by several submarines. It was now up to *Bahála Ná* and her thoroughly tired crew to undertake the mission against the mysterious and dangerous Q-boats.

There was no problem recruiting and reenforcing the crew. Bob was skipper with Fermin as pilot. Gary manned the forward machine gun, a heavy and efficient Japanese Nambu. Corporal Tomas handled the forward twin .50 caliber turret on the starboard side, while young Abundio handled the after turret on the port side. Mama Rosalia and Papa Alibongbong took over the rusted, almost worn out 37 mm. antitank gun on the afterdeck. Blas had recruited an experienced Filipino mechanic to help him on the triple Packards, a smiling lad from Luzon by the name of Demiterio Augustine de Garcia, whose pleasant exterior concealed a ferocious love of battle. The radio operator was a quiet little Filipino named Manuelito, who had been trained by Bob. In addition they took aboard a squad of guerrillas, all picked men, led by tough Sergeant Nazareno, whose entire family had been wiped out by the Hapons on an island off Luzon. These "Bolo Boys" were the guerrilla elite.

A Japanese naval flag was procured for the boat. Canvas was painted white, with the red meatball insignia in the

191

center, and placed on the foredeck and atop the cabin. Japanese naval caps were issued to the crew.

They waited in the shadows of late afternoon for orders from the colonel. Just as the sun was gone the message came. As Bob conned the PT through the twisted, mangrove-bordered channel in the darkness under the directions of Fermin he felt the first drops of rain strike his face, and then he heard the drops striking the windshield in front of his face. By the time they were clear of the channel the rain was hissing steadily into the dark waters.

18 . . .

Bahála Ná crept through the dripping darkness like a cat stalking an unseen mouse. The boat barely had steerageway on her, and the Packards seemed to purr under the skilled hands of Blas and Demiterio. Bob wiped the rainwater from his face. His Japanese naval cap was thoroughly soaked. Somewhere off to starboard were some of the small islands that guarded the entrance to Balayan Bay. Manila was about one hundred miles to the north. They had swiftly crossed rainswept Verde Passage under the cover of darkness and had not seen an enemy patrol boat or any other craft.

Bob glanced at Fermin. The pilot was perfectly calm. "Right a little," he said. Bob turned the wheel. He himself could see nothing out in the wet and windy darkness. He could see Gary's back where he bent over his tarpaulin-covered Nambu. He was ready to fire at an instant's warning. Bob glanced back over his right shoulder. He could just make out Corporal Tomas in his turret. The others were all at battle stations.

"Right a little," said Fermin.

Bob nodded. The boat lifted and fell in the swell running into the bay. The current was strong. He wondered if the makeshift patches on the hull were holding. While they were rescuing dunked aviators they had had to keep the pumps going most of the time.

"Steady," said Fermin.

The pounding the PT had taken out in the open sea hadn't helped her any. Bob knew she was good for about one more job. After that she'd be a total loss, even if she did manage to get out of Balayan Bay. He didn't have much faith in their getting out of the bay. Now and then the thought of those deadly Q-boats, packed with explosives and manned by two completely fanatical Japanese whose greatest glory was to die for the Emperor and Dai Nippon, didn't set too well. He knew Bledsoe had alerted the Luzon guerrilla *borobas* in the Balayan Bay area that *Bahála Ná* was coming to deal with the Q-boats. Bob didn't have much faith in their helping the PT boat and its crew. It was going into a hornet's nest, and the Hapons would be more touchy and nervous than usual what with The Aid due any day. Carrier-plane attacks had already plastered some of the area, but no one knew how many, if any, of the Q-boats had been destroyed or damaged. Well, it wouldn't be long before *Bahála Ná* and her crew found out.

"Right! Right! Right!" said Fermin sharply.

The bottom of the boat scraped lightly. "I thought you knew these waters!" snapped Bob.

"That is only a sandbar," said Fermin patiently.

"We can't even afford sandbars!" said Bob.

Fermin looked at him. "It is necessary to cross it," he said.

Bob bit his lip. His nerves were ragged. "I'm sorry, Fermin," he said.

"It is nothing, my friend. I do not feel too well myself," Fermin peered through the darkness. It was thicker up there. Then Bob could make out the narrow channel between the little island and the larger one that Fermin had told him about. He eased the boat at dead slow speed into the channel, feeling the brush rubbing against the sides. Vines hung down and trailed along the wet decks.

"Now," said the pilot.

Bob cut the engines. She drifted gently as Gary and Papa Alibongbong made her fast to overhanging trees.

"What now?" said Gary over his shoulder.

"We wait for light," said Bob.

"There is a moon," said Corporal Tomas.

Gary looked up. "You kidding, Tomas?"

"The rain will soon stop," said Papa Alibongbong. "It is a late moon. If the rain stops, we will have the light for an hour or so."

"Then we don't have to wait for the dawn," said Bob.

No one spoke. The very thought of what they were committed to do was too nerve-racking to discuss.

"Chow?" said Blas.

"You're on," said Gary.

"I knew you'd respond," said Blas. "We got Mindoro chicken."

"What's that?" said Fermin.

"Canned Vienna sausages," said Blas. He grinned. "Under *glass*, of course!"

"Listen!" said Corporal Tomas.

Faintly through the darkness came the throbbing of an engine. There were no lights on *Bahála Ná*, and she was faded and discolored so that she blended in perfectly with the surrounding trees and brush of the shore.

The sound of the engine came closer. It was either a fishing boat or a patrol boat. The rain pattered on the decks of the PT boat. The water slapped against her patched sides. The mooring lines creaked as the boat felt the tug of the current sweeping through the narrow gut between the two islands.

The boat was now just offshore. The engine thudded

and echoed back from the shore. Bob could see the faintest of bluish lights moving above the water, rising and falling with the lift and drop of the boat. There was no way of telling what she was.

There was a sudden stab of light from a searchlight aboard the strange craft. "Keep your faces out of the light!" snapped Bob. The moving finger of vivid light worked along the shore. The raindrops and wet foliage glistened in the light. The finger reached the narrow channel and stopped, moving up and down to examine a shattered, rusted hulk lying halfway in and out of the water. She was scarred by fire and shell. Bob bent his head and prayed. The engine increased power and the thudding noise echoed through the channel. Bob risked a look. The searchlight had flicked out toward the open bay as the patrol boat passed the channel and it swung sharply in again to pick up the shoreline beyond the channel.

"Close, too close," breathed Fermin. He rested his head against the side of the cockpit. "I have been in this war too long," he added quietly. "It is not the same anymore, Roberto."

"I know," said Bob. "Go below and get some chow. I'll stand watch, Fermin."

The rain pattered down and dripped from the overhanging trees. The faint sound of the patrol-boat engine came across the water. Bob was afraid, unsure of himself, and well he might be, at his age, despite his many and varied experiences in the war, to be in command of even such a small craft as a PT boat. He tried to remember the skill of Lieutenant Carney, who had been skipper of the PT boat Bob had temporarily served on in the Solomons. Carney had been one of the best in the business at the various duties of barge-bopping, patrolling, sea-air rescue, and running in supplies and equipment for the coast watchers. He tried to remember all the tricks of the trade.

"A man can only do his best," the voice said behind Bob. It was Corporal Tomas. "A man does not fight merely to win. Even in losing something is accomplished, Roberto."

Bob nodded. Somehow the tough guerrilla seemed to have sensed how Bob felt. Bob had a good crew and *Bahála Ná,* despite her shortcomings, still packed a giant's wallop in a pygmy's build.

The rain drizzled out. Only the trees dripped. It was very quiet out on the bay. Now and then the faint and ghostly sound of an engine would drift across the bay. The sky was still dark. Bob shrugged. He might have known there would be no moon. He went below to eat, leaving Fermin on watch. When Bob came on deck again, Fermin pointed to the sky. The faint, ever so faint, light of the moon was showing.

Before the moonlight flooded the bay *Bahála Ná* was eased out of her hiding place. Bob steered her toward the still unseen shore. "The Q-boats will be located along the creeks and *ilogs,*" said Fermin.

Bob nodded. There was nothing to do to get ready. They had been ready for hours. He let Fermin steer and picked up a pair of powerful Japanese night glasses he had found in a locker. He scanned the darkness of the shore. Sometimes he picked up a faint light. The sound of the Packards and the wash and gurgle of the water at the bows and patched flanks of the boat seemed inordinately loud, but then the Japanese were used to hearing the engines of patrol and fishing boats out in the bay. *Bahála Ná* still had a good turn of speed if necessary, although Blas hadn't guaranteed how long he could keep it up.

Gary looked back at Bob. Bob grinned and nodded. He knew Gary was as frightened as he was, but Gary was only trying to reassure him. He needed a lot of reassuring.

The moonlight traveled across the distant hills and the

197

far side of the bay was touched with its slanted light. The east shore was still dark in shadow. Bob's glasses picked up something unnatural on the shore. It took him a few minutes to realize that they must be fuel tanks set among the trees and well camouflaged, at least from the air. The Japanese always had been camouflage happy.

Bahála Ná crept closer and closer just ahead of the full light of the moon. It was too easy. Bob looked back over his shoulder. He could see a faint moving light out on the water. He looked around again at the tanks. "What kind of engines do those Q-boats have?" he asked the pilot.

"The colonel said they were converted automobile engines."

"Then they use gasoline for fuel," said Bob thoughtfully.

"Of course," said the pilot. He looked closely at Bob. "Why?"

"Never mind now," said Bob.

The moonlight was almost across the bay, touching the tree-shrouded islands and beginning to glint a little from the choppy waves.

"There!" said Gary. He had eyes like a cat. He pointed a little to port.

Bob raised the glasses. He looked into the wide mouth of a tree-bordered creek. Heavily festooned camouflage nets hung down from the trees or stretched across the open area above the creek. The light was a little clearer now. He could distinguish something looking like enormously fat crocodiles lying in the shallow water or resting on the muddy shores. An icy feeling came into his body. They were small boats about fourteen feet long, almost fully decked, and painted a dull indistinguishable color. *The Q-boats!*

"Boat coming up fast astern!" said Abundio.

"Play it cool," said Bob. He eased the helm a little, steering away from the mouth of the creek. He looked back over his shoulder to see the wide V of the boat's prow spreading a whiskery curl of whitish phosphorescent water to each side. She was moving in fast! A signal light began to dot and dash. Bob twirled the wheel and headed parallel to the shore. A searchlight stabbed out and touched the canvas that hung over the side of the PT boat, reaching the garish red meatball in the center of the dingy white canvas. The signal flicked on and on. If the boat closed with them, the game would be up. Bob could see a manned gun on her foredeck.

"Gary!" he cried. "I'm turning to meet her at slow speed! When I give full throttle, you'd better take care of that deck gun of theirs!"

"Aye, aye, Skipper!" said Gary. He patted his quaint-looking Japanese naval cap more firmly on his head.

Bob twirled the wheel sharply, and the PT boat turned toward the oncoming patrol boat. He could see the men moving about on her decks. She was about the same length as *Baháła Ná* but much more heavily built and armed, and she was fast closing the gap toward the slowly moving PT boat. Bob's throat went dry. If they opened up first, they'd cream the deck of the PT boat, aiming, no doubt, for the cockpit. The moonlight was bright on the water. The searchlight flicked out. A siren sounded above the sound of the engines. The gap closed to fifty yards. There was no reason to dally. Bob suddenly threw the throttles all the way forward and there was an instantaneous response from the three powerful Packards. The surge nearly hurled Bob to the deck of the cockpit. Fermin steadied him. Bob gripped the wheel and steered so as to pass the port side of the oncoming boat. The gun on her forward deck flashed. Bob winced and his head seemed to sink down between his shoulders. The flat crack of the gun carried across the water and something rushed just over the cockpit. Bob glanced astern. A shimmering foam-white water tree stood up from the dark surface of the bay.

Gary opened fire with the heavy Nambu. The tracers arced toward the patrol boat, and then seemed to be swallowed in her bows. They raised and a hail of slugs swept the foredeck. Corporal Tomas and Abundio did not wait for orders. Four .50 caliber machine guns flashed and stuttered, sweeping the small pilothouse of the Japanese craft, shattering glass and ripping woodwork. A man fell out of the open side door and rolled across the deck and over the side to splash into the water. Mama Rosalia's 37mm. barked as Bob slewed *Bahála Ná* with a great creaming of her wide wake. The deck gun was out of action, swinging back and forth as the boat went out of control. Three Japanese ran along the splintered deck to man the gun, but Abundio caught them at a point-blank range of fifty feet and the slugs literally swept them over the side. A machine gun flashed from the afterdeck of the boat. Slugs smashed into the cabin of the PT boat. Glass shattered. Gary adjusted his aim. The Nambu silenced the machine gun. The patrol boat lost way and wallowed in the chop. Bob slewed *Bahála Ná* and drove in for the kill. "Aim at the waterline!" he yelled.

The six guns lowered their aim and stitched across the waterline tearing ragged and gaping holes. Papa Alibong-bong reached down into a gunny sack and took out two of Mama Rosalia's deadly Shelby tubing grenades. Bob interpreted his move. He steered the racing PT boat in a wide and sweeping half circle, then shot along her side, hardly twenty feet away. The moonlight shone on the first grenade as it sailed through the air and struck atop the pilothouse. It exploded. The walls bulged out, and the structure collapsed like wet cardboard. The second grenade fell through a hole in the side of the cabin over the engine room. There was a stunning crash and explosion of orange-red flame and thick smoke, and the top of the cabin was lifted off by an invisible hand. The patrol craft suddenly listed. She sagged over on her side. She sank deeper. As *Bahála Ná* raced for the mouth of the creek, the patrol boat went under with a gurgling rush, leaving nothing on the surface but fragments of raw splintered wood.

There was no need for stealth now. The vicious sound of the guns and the shattering explosions had echoed and reechoed across the bay. Lights flicked on all along the shore. A searchlight stabbed out its beam toward the oncoming PT boat. A gun flashed beside it and a spout of water arose right in front of the high-riding flared bows of the PT boat. Bob twirled the wheel and *Bahála Ná* heeled over, almost as though she would roll under. A spout of water rose right where she had been seconds before.

A small patrol boat gathered way. *Bahála Ná* snapped at her with gunfire. She lost way and wallowed in the surf. A flicker of fire danced along her deck. It flared up. Men dived over the side like clumsy frogs. Then her tanks let go and she exploded, scattering flaming debris across the waters.

Bob grinned as he looked again toward the creek, and then the grin faded. Half a dozen low-lying craft were moving swiftly out of the darkened mouth of the creek, wallowing a little as they reached the surf line. They were heading directly toward *Bahála Ná!*

"Q-boats!" yelled Bob.

The chattering of Gary's heavy Nambu echoed Bob's yell. Tracers skipped across the water and ricocheted, some of them bounding clear over the tiny fleet that was heading for the PT boat. If one of them struck *Bahála Ná,* there wouldn't be enough left afloat to make a small-scale replica of her. They were literally moving mines that could destroy a cruiser if they could ram her.

Gary's slugs drove into the lead boat. Splinters flew. Suddenly the boat erupted in a shattering crash, taking three others with her. Mud and water cascaded high into the air and rained down upon the PT boat. Bob took advantage of the cover and confusion to swing *Bahála Ná* to port, allowing Corporal Tomas to open up with his twin .50's into the remaining Q-boats.

Somewhere on shore a Chicago piano opened up with a *poomp-poomp-poomp-poomp*, gobbling like an enraged turkey and scattering orange-blue tracers across the water. Her projectiles tore right over the few remaining Q-boats. One of them shattered as its charge let go. The slugs rose and tore through *Bahála Ná*. Corporal Tomas bravely fired directly at the flickering Japanese gunfire and then jerked suddenly. He fell lifelessly over the side of his turret with the smoking twin .50's swinging aimlessly back and forth as *Bahála Ná* twisted and turned out toward the open water. Gary leaped back from his gun as the Chicago piano chewed the makeshift deck almost at his feet. A beam let go, and the heavy Nambu tilted over the side with Gary hanging desperately to it.

"Let it go, you knothead!" screamed Bob.

Gary dived for cover. Bob swung *Bahála Ná* from side to side. The Nambu snapped from its mounting and plunged over the side, taking a ragged square of decking with it.

"More Q-boats!" shouted Fermin.

This time they were coming from farther along the shoreline. There were at least ten of them. *Bahála Ná* turned away. More Q-boats came out of the first creek like deadly insects trying to get in a lethal sting.

"It's no use!" shrieked the pilot. "There are too many of

them! We must retreat!" He reached for the wheel. Bob shoved him aside. Fermin struck at him and reached again for the wheel. He was surprisingly strong for one of his slight build. Bob smashed a fist against the side of Fermin's head. The pilot whipped out his bolo. Gary rose over the side of the cockpit and swung his heavy automatic pistol sideways. The flat side of the barrel housing struck just above Fermin's ear, and he went down, his bolo clattering on the deck. Gary jumped into the cockpit and dumped the crazed Filipino down the ladder.

It was too late to turn aside. *Bahála Ná* plunged in among the low-lying Q-boats. Two of them were smashed under her forefoot. Their charges did not go off. The surging bow wave swamped two more of them. They hit another a glancing blow and were only fifty feet past her when she exploded. Bob had a fleeting vision of one of her doomed crew seemingly floating up spread-eagled through the air, firmly supported by the gas of the explosion. Water and mud showered down on *Bahála Ná*, coating her from stem to stern.

Machine guns chattered from Abundio's turret, and another Q-boat exploded. The bay was now alight with moonlight, and smoke hung over the water from the many explosions and from the roaring, chattering guns of both sides. *Bahála Ná* swung out wide and caught a savage burst from the Chicago piano that shattered Mama Rosalia's 37mm. and wounded Papa Alibongbong in the arm. She dragged the wounded man aside and cradled him in her thick arms, protecting his body with hers.

Gary climbed over the rear of the cockpit and with the help of two guerrillas pulled Corporal Tomas' body from the turret. Gary settled himself into the turret and opened up on the shoreline after his ammunition supply had been replenished by a guerrilla.

Offshore the choppy water was thick with Q-boats and

other craft trying to get close to the buzzing, killing mosquito boat that was battling single-handed in Balayan Bay. Fermin was right, thought Bob, as he used evasive tactics to avoid gunfire and the oncoming Q-boats. There *were* too many of them and they *should* retreat. There was only one solution. "Get Blas on deck!" he yelled at a guerrilla. A moment later the big cook was in the cockpit.

"Aye, aye, Skipper!" He looked about at the havoc on the deck of *Bahála Ná.* "Looks as if all the fun has been up here!"

"Can you fire those torpedoes?" yelled Bob over his shoulder.

"I know *how* to fire them! I won't guarantee they'll fire!"

"We'll take a chance on that! I'm aiming for the first creek. Fire the starboard torpedo first! I'll raise my hand to alert you. When I chop it down, you fire! Understand?"

"Aye, aye, sir!"

"Jump and make it so then!"

Bahála Ná turned obediently toward the first creek. One of her Packards was running unevenly. All they had to do was to lose power. Bob sickened at the thought. He aimed for the creek mouth, roaring within fifty feet of several rocking Q-boats. He saw the camouflaged tanks. Two hundred yards . . . one hundred and fifty . . . one hundred yards. Bob raised his right hand, steering with his left. They were almost within the mouth of the creek, and he shuddered a little as he saw the massed Q-boats with men running about them, some of them firing rifles and automatic weapons at the oncoming PT boat. Bob lined up the metal windshield base with the radio antenna like a gunsight as he had often seen Lieutenant Carney do. The tanks grew in size. At the last possible second Bob chopped his right hand down hard.

19 . . .

Ziiing-pung! The dated Mark VIII torpedo lunged from the tube. Bob twirled the wheel. *Bahála Ná* swung hard over, skidding across the muddy waters. She slewed toward a row of mangroves. Her bottom scraped, and one of the Packards rose in roaring pitch. Bob cut it off. *Bahála Ná* had lost one of her three props.

The torpedo porpoised out of the water and plunged down again, scattering spray high in the air. She struck a moored Q-boat sideways, and it immediately exploded. The torpedo slithered up on the muddy shore and arrowed toward the nearest fuel tank. At the last possible second she struck something, and a fraction of a second before exploding she hurled herself sideways through the nearest tank. WHOOMF! The tank bellied out at the side, and the top came off like a jack-in-the-box. A brilliant orange-yellow gush of flame soared upward, and then the explosion thudded into the atmosphere to set every echo on the bay into life. Tank after tank let go in fiery sympathy.

Bahála Ná was racing ahead of the flame and gas that poured from the mouth of the creek. Q-boat after Q-boat exploded, hurling wood and men high into the air to meet the roaring maelstrom of flame and gas that filled the air above the creek and the shore. Out of the darkness of the shore a heavy gun flamed. Water spouted just ahead of *Bahála Ná*. The gun flamed again and something struck abaft the mast, ripping through the roof of the cabin and scattering plywood and the after .50 caliber gun turret into the sea. Abundio was hurled to the afterdeck where only Mama Rosalia's strong arm saved the unconscious young Filipino from going over the side into the churning wake. A flicker of flame danced along the splintered wood and was batted out by blankets wielded by some of the guerrillas. A third and fourth shot struck the water in front of the PT boat as Bob swung her sharply to port. A cascade of water crashed down on the boat.

Bob looked ahead. There was another creek there, much narrower than the one they had already attacked. He could see Q-boats bunched in the mouth of it. The shoreline was alive with flickering gun flashes, and the gap between the shore and *Bahála Ná* was a fiery display of arcing tracers.

"Blas!" screamed Bob.

The big cook had anticipated Bob's command. He crouched by the port forward torpedo tube. A trickle of blood ran down his pale face. Bob raised his right arm. Vibration had set up in the hull of the wracked PT boat. She shuddered as though in deep pain, running on two props, and it was evident that one of them at least had either been badly bent or had lost a blade. Tracers skipped and bounced from the water and soared over *Bahála Ná*. Something struck high on the bows, tearing off what remained of the forward deck. It was flung over the side like the lid of a sardine can, dragging in the water, throwing the boat off course. Bob struggled with the wheel to correct the course. Once again he raised his arm, and when he looked toward the creek, he realized there was hardly time enough left to fire. The radio antenna was gone. He could only guess. He chopped down his arm.

ZIIING-PUNG! The deadly tin fish hit the water, throwing up a shower of spray. She burrowed through the bullet-torn water. She porpoised a little just in front of a group of Q-boats. Screaming Japanese plunged over the sides of their little craft. The Mark VIII plunged back into the water leaving a creaming wake. She struck alongside a rickety wharf and exploded, hurling the wharf, Q-boats, men, and gear high into the smoky air. The roaring of the explosion slammed back and forth, and the shock of it struck back at *Bahála Ná* as she was slewed to port. She hit something in the water and shuddered violently from stem to stern. The piece of decking was torn free.

She was so close to the shoreline the Japanese gunners could hardly miss, illuminated as she was by flames and the bright moonlight. Her starboard side was literally chewed through from stem to stern. Three guerrillas died in the hail of slugs. Something exploded in the engine room. Flames leaped up through the gaping hole in the cabin top. A heavy shell smashed into the water to starboard and the resultant deluge neatly put out the fire and also shielded *Bahála Ná* long enough to get away from the deadly and devastating machine-gun fire from the shore.

She was running on the one remaining engine, and she had been mortally injured. Blas dropped below and started the pumps, but they could not keep up with the inflow of water from the many holes and long gashes in the hull for very long. A small patrol boat cut in on the slowly moving PT boat and was driven off by Gary and his twin .50's. The patrol boat went dead in the water and was left astern as Gary ran out the last of his ammunition. *Bahála Ná* was now defenseless.

Bob steered for the many small islands near the mouth

of the bay. There was a far-out chance they might be able to beach her and find a hiding place on the islands. By dawn the bay would be alive with bloodthirsty Japanese hunting for the madmen who had destroyed their Q-boat fleet. Flames still flared up against the sky, and a pall of thick black smoke hung over the bay. At least the smoke helped conceal *Bahála Ná* as she crept off to die.

They grounded her just off one of the islands and waded ashore with the dead and wounded. Bob came back to the beach as the moon died.

Blas stood there watching the stricken boat. "She was a fighter," he said. "She paid her way, kid. The only thing that's keeping her up is the bottom. The Lord alone knows how we got her this far."

Bob eyed the shattered hulk. Her back must be broken by now as she swung back and forth in the wash of the surf. She was pitted and gashed, scarred and smoke-stained. "Where's Eugene?" he said.

Blas pointed to the boat. "He didn't make it," he said sadly.

Bob looked toward the distant fires. "What do you think?" he said quietly.

"They'll be here by dawn," said Blas.

Gary limped up to them. "Abundio just died," he said.

They stood there with the surf washing about their bare feet. *Bahála Ná* creaked and groaned. The moon was gone now. In a little while the dawn would come.

"We've still got our side arms," said Blas. "They won't take *me* alive."

They sat down on the shore with their backs against trees and their weapons across their laps. The thick darkness after the passing of the moon began to thin. There was a tinge of faint pearly gray in the eastern sky. Fires glowed across the bay.

208

"We'd better get under cover," said Blas.

They stood up. A rushing sound came through the air, followed by distant thudding noise and out at sea, in Verde Passage, they could see flickering, stabbing light. They whirled as crashing explosion after crashing explosion thundered across the bay. Spouts of water shot up. Trees were uprooted and flung high into the air. Again and again the rushing sound came through the air as though gigantic and invisible partridges were homing in on the bay shore. Just as the dawn light grew, there was a steady droning noise high in the sky. Formation after formation of planes came in from the direction of the South China Sea.

"You know something?" said Gary casually. "That's *The Aid*, fellows. Those are carrier aircraft or I never went to an aircraft identification class on the good ol' *Logie* under Chief West."

The planes began to dive, spraying the shoreline and every installation with gunfire. Bombs crumped on the ground, mingling their explosions and damage with those of the unseen warships that were plastering Balayan Bay.

By sunup it was old hat to the weary, battered, hungry, and completely fed up crew of *Bahála Ná,* or what remained of the composite group that *Bahála Ná* had had as a crew.

Gary looked at Bob. "And you didn't think you could handle her," he said. "Man, you sure underestimated yourself."

"I'll buy that," said Blas.

Bob grinned wearily. "You know, I got so busy I forgot to be afraid." He looked out at the wreck of *Bahála Ná*. "At that, I think it was *Bahála Ná* herself who really did the job, not us."

"Amen to that," said Blas. "Look!"

An American destroyer was feeling her way into the bay. Behind her was a covey of PT boats, spreading creaming wakes, alert for signs of the enemy. The offshore fire had stopped, although the planes were still working over the Japanese installations. The destroyer swung a little closer to the island, and the three *Bahála Ná* men ran up and down, waving their arms. They knew they were being closely observed from the destroyer. A motor whaler plunged into the water and raced for the shore with half a dozen seamen in her armed to the teeth.

The whaler neared the shore and cut her engine. "Any of you speak English?" yelled a mean-looking bosun's mate.

"Some!" yelled Gary.

"Drop those guns! Who are you?"

"We're guerrillas!" yelled Blas.

The bosun's mate looked at the coxswain of the whaler. "Can you beat that?" he said. "He thinks he's King Kong."

The whaler touched ground, and the seamen splashed ashore. In fifteen minutes they had rounded up what remained of the crew of *Bahála Ná*. The motor whaler headed back out to the lean, efficient-looking destroyer. "Look at that hulk," said the coxswain as he pointed to *Bahála Ná*. "Must have been busted up when the Japs took over the Philippines. It's been there a long time from the looks of it."

A PT boat swung toward them and slowed down to idling speed. "We're going in for those Q-boats!" called an officer importantly through a megaphone. "Can you locate them for us?"

Gary looked up. "Sure, sir!" he yelled back. "But you're a little late! Go on ahead though! You might find a *couple* we missed! Be careful of your paint, sir! It's awfully smoky over there!"

The officer was still staring with a puzzled look at the whaler as it was made fast to the falls and hoisted aboard the destroyer.

Gary, Blas, and Bob got out on the deck of the destroyer under the curious eyes of the men there. A lieutenant commander came up to the *Bahála Ná* crew. "Colonel Bledsoe told us to look out for you. Frankly, we did not expect to find you."

"Frankly, sir," said Bob, "we didn't expect to be here."

The officer smiled. "Is there anything we can do for you?"

Gary raised his head. "We could use some good chow, sir."

"All you want!" The officer looked at a seaman. "What's for chow today, Loomis?"

"Vienna Sausage, sir," said the seaman.

The hungry look faded from Gary's face. *"Bahála ná,"* he said.

The destroyer moved slowly into the bay. The PT boats fanned out, eagerly looking for targets. They wouldn't find many in Balayan Bay, but they would find plenty of them in other places—Batangas Bay at Tabangao, Janao Bay near Anilao, and between Mabini and Bauan. They would get all of them. The Navy surface and aircraft were softening up the great island of Luzon before the land forces came to liberate the Philippines. The Bamboo War was almost over. It was now the turn of the powerful United States forces who did not have to fight with brass curtain-rod bullets, barbed wire telegraph lines, iron-pipe cannon and tuba gasoline. It was the beginning of the end for the Japanese forces in the Philippines. *Bahála ná!*

Glossary

abacá fiber	Manila hemp
adobo	barbecue chicken and pork with rice
The Aid	supplies from MacArthur in Australia
amanatto	sugared red beans
amtrac	amphibious tractor
anas	malaria mosquitoes
bagakay	bamboo shoots, poisonous
bagool	half a coconut shell
bahála ná	come what may
banca	boat hollowed from a log, often with an outrigger
banig	woven sleeping mat
banzai	victory cry of Japanese warriors
barong tagalog	embroidered shirt of filmy cloth, worn outside of trousers
baroto	dugout canoe, larger than a banca
barrio	settlement, village
BC	Bureau of Constabulary, Filipino police under Japanese rule
bodega	warehouse, storeroom
bojong	conch shell with a hole in it; a bird
boroba	a guerrilla force
bueno	good
buqwee	to leave in a hurry; to evacuate
caba-caba	small dugout canoe

213

carabao	water buffalo
Chibasco	solid wall of rain a mile wide, with high winds in it
Chicago piano	a pompom, an automatic machine cannon
chop-chop	quickly, promptly
cogongrass	a high, very sharp-edged grass
daifuki mochi	rice cakes stuffed with bean paste
Dai Nippon	Japan
gracias	thank you
Hapons	the Japanese
ilog	river
Kalibapi	Filipino secret societies
kinkie lamp	a torch fueled by coconut oil
kuru bark	from the *kuru* tree
¿No es verdad?	Isn't it?
Los muertos no hablan, amigos.	The dead do not speak, friends.
Oi vey!	Oh, my!
pechay	lettuce cabbage
poto sicle	baked rice bread
prau	Malayan canoe
¿Quién sabe?	Who knows?
sawali	woven split bamboo
Sigi legi, ho!	Get going, get on the ball!
SOP	Standard Operating Procedure
suak	sharpened bamboo splinters
tuba	fermented sap of various palms used to make alcohol
yokan	sweet bean jelly

Bibliography

Hernandez, Al, *Bahála Na, Come What May: The Story of Mission ISRM* (I Shall Return, MacArthur), an Army-Navy Intelligence Mission in the Pacific, as told to Dixon Earle; foreword by Douglas MacArthur. Howell-North Books, 1961.

Keats, John, *They Fought Alone.* J. B. Lippincott, 1963; Pocket Books, Inc., 1965.

Volckmann, Russel W., *We Remained: Three Years Behind the Enemy Lines in the Philippines.* W. W. Norton & Company, Inc., 1954.

Wolfert, Ira, *American Guerrilla in the Philippines.* Simon and Schuster, Inc., 1945.

Biography of Gordon D. Shirreffs

GORDON D. SHIRREFFS was born in Chicago, Illinois, where he attended grammar school and high school. While in high school he was active in R.O.T.C., track, wrestling, and rifle-shooting. After leaving high school, he worked at various jobs, his best memories being of two summer sessions spent as a hand on a fifty-foot sailing ketch cruising the Great Lakes. Later he enlisted in the Illinois National Guard and started work at the Union Tank Car Company of Chicago. At night he studied at Northwestern University.

In September, 1940, he was called to active military service as a sergeant in the antiaircraft artillery. He was promoted to second lieutenant in January, 1941. During the war years he served in Alaska and throughout the Aleutian campaign, later serving as a transport commander on a Norwegian ship, the *Fridtjof Nansen,* in Mediterranean waters. He was honorably discharged in December, 1945, with the rank of captain. He went back to work at the Union Tank Car Company and reentered Northwestern University, Medill School of Journalism, to study professional fiction-writing. From 1946 until 1952 he worked as a salesman, booking agent, and demonstrator. He also had short stories published in boys' magazines and in adventure magazines.

Mr. Shirreffs moved to California in 1952, and bought a home in Granada Hills in the San Fernando Valley, where he took up full-time professional writing. At the present time he has sold over two hundred short stories, *novelas,* and novelettes, fifty-seven full-length books, eighteen in the juvenile category, two movies, *The Lonesome Trail* and *Oregon Passage, The Galvanized Yankee* on *Playhouse 90,* based on his book *Massacre Creek,* and two other television plays. Books and stories have been printed in Canada, Australia, the United Kingdom, Denmark, Norway, Sweden, and Italy. Three of his boys' stories have been printed in Braille. Others have appeared in *The Boys' Life Book of Scout Stories, Boys' Life Treasury, Teen-Age Frontier Stories, Young in the Saddle,* and *Frontiers to Explore, Teacher's Edition.*

His hobbies are Western and Civil War history, archery, rifle and pistol marksmanship, and model-making, and he has acted as technical adviser and archer in movies. One of his most interesting hobbies is playing the tenor drum in the San Fernando–Burbank Fire Department Bagpipe Band. He is an active member of the Veterans of Foreign Wars.

He and his wife have a daughter, Carole Alice, and a son, Brian Allen.